rain on the leaves

Rain on the leaves

RICHARD BLANEY

© 2024 by Richard Blaney

All rights reserved. This book or any portion thereof may not be reproduced or used in any manner whatsoever without the express written permission of the publisher except for the use of brief quotations in a book review.

Paperback ISBN: 9798822946637

the wall

Father John, a retired Jesuit priest, observed his Slazenger golf ball nestled under a clump of sea grass. He closed the face of his wedge and jumped the ball down the fairway turf. It was the par five 18th hole at Lahinch Golf Club. It gave him a good chance to up and down the green.

James Flaherty, the American golfer, noticed the father's clerical collar above a tattered buttonhole. "Nice shot." Father John nodded with a sly smile. James and Robert Neill walked down the fairway for their second shots.

"That was amazing," James said.

"The good father is a fine golfer," Neill replied. "Since his retirement, he plays at least three times a week."

James asked, "Why doesn't he wear something else than that raggedy frock?"

"Poverty," came the reply.

"How can he afford to play?"

"Charity mostly. You see, our Irish friends pay annual dues at two hundred pounds. Father John, one hundred. The club makes up for it by overcharging tourists."

"Yeah," Flaherty said. "I paid eighty for today. It's worth it, though. What do you think I should hit?"

"Do you carry a four-iron?"

"Yes."

"Hit a low draw for run-out."

James' ball ran to within a hundred yards from the green. Robert hit a five-iron closer. Father John slapped a mid-iron even closer. James three-putted for a bogey; Robert two-putted for a par, and the good Father chipped in for a birdie. They shook hands and went into the clubhouse.

Robert bought two Guinness' for Flaherty and himself, and Father John had a Bulmers on the house. Robert took a swig and said, "Mr. Flaherty. How do you like our course?"

"Wonderful. Especially the hole where the tee was on the beach. I hit a nice three-wood, but it went into that huge bunker. I never before had to climb down a ladder to get to the ball!"

"Like a big black hole," Robert said. "But you got out of it well. What did you hit?"

"A pitching wedge."

"And a birdie, as well. Bravo!" He raised his glass for a toast.

"Charming," James said.

Father John left for another table without a word. James said, "Being from Canada, what brought you here?"

"My wife is from Omagh, and she wanted to return after we retired. She's a chemical engineer, and I'm electrical."

"Then you have done well, my friend. Where do you live now?"

"Limerick. We have a nice house and thoroughly enjoy the city. Where are you staying?"

"Limerick. The Woodfield House."

"Oh. The new place north of the city."

"It's perfect. Close to the airport and situated in a residential neighborhood."

The Canadian wiped his chin. "When are you going home? And where is home?"

"South Carolina. I'm leaving day after tomorrow."

"I thought I heard the accent."

"Tell me, Robert. What about the goats? I've never seen goats grazing on a golf course."

"Legend and superstition. You see, it used to be that sheep, goats, and donkeys grazed here. Then the committee banned all but the goats in 1919. The villagers didn't like it at first, but got used to it. The goats still graze."

"What about superstition?"

"One day the barometer next to the clubhouse broke, but it never got fixed. In time they realized that the goats were a natural barometer. If they're out grazing, it won't rain, but if they stay close to the clubhouse, better put on your raingear."

"That is superstitious." James swallowed the rest of his beer. "Charming."

"My wife should be here soon to pick me up." Robert shook James' hand. "I enjoyed your company, Mr. Flaherty, and the round. Thank you, and God bless."

Mrs. Neill arrived and came into the clubhouse. She wore her age well, stunning black hair and brown Irish eyes. After introductions, she said, "South Carolina, huh? We went to Myrtle Beach one year in June, like now. Enjoyed it. The beach is so wide and smooth, it was spectacular."

"I'm from Columbia in the middle of the state." He sighed and peered out for a last look at Lahinch. I felt like I was in heaven, he thought, but maybe I was on the moon with the craters and ocean. "Hope to see you again."

* * *

The hotel's car park was almost full. James struggled for a place at the back; squeezing into a tight space, with the steering wheel on the right side, it was harder to judge. He walked into the front door and saw the redheaded Aileen still working the front desk. "Mr. Flaherty. How did you get around?"

"Very well."

She smiled. "Did the club pair you?"

"With two fine gentlemen."

"Perfect."

He heard steady conversation in the bar. He wanted to join in with the locals and liked carousing outside on the terrace. He said to Aileen, "Working late, are yuh?"

"Oh my! I didn't realize the time. I'm just finishing up. I don't want to go home just yet, and I don't wanna be alone in there, indicating the bar. You mind if I join you?"

"Delighted."

"I'll be here finishing up."

Twenty minutes later, he saw her approach. "Thank you for joining me."

He rose and pulled back the chair at the table. She pointed to the booth. "Do you mind if we sit over there?"

Lianne came with the burger he had ordered. "Aileen!" She smiled. "You'll be with us a wee bit longer; what'll you have?"

"I think a Coca-Cola."

James almost dropped his glass. "You're American. And from the South, too."

"Statesboro, Georgia. You're from South Carolina, I know."

"What are you doing here?"

"Gettin' a master's at Shannon College."

"Shannon College?"

"Hotel Management and Hospitality School."

James had to swallow some black stuff and wipe the foam off his lips. "What kind of Masters?"

Aileen smiled. "Global Hospitality Management and Intercultural Communication."

"That's a mouthful," he said. "What are you going to do with that?"

"Hopefully travel and work."

"Interesting."

Aileen smiled again. "I have a degree in communications from Georgia Southern. I thought I could put it to better use."

She sipped her Coke, then continued, "Did you go to USC?"

"Yes."

"Your major?"

"International Studies."

"We have something in common. May I be as bold to ask if you are married?"

"No. I don't think I ever will. I'm too wrapped up in my business."

"What business is that?"

"I own a wholesale seafood business."

"Interesting."

James looked into her eyes. "And what about you, Aileen? Did you ever consider it?"

She sighed. "When I was a junior, I met a senior in ROTC. We fell hard. He graduated, got commissioned, and was assigned to Vietnam. He wanted us to get married, but I wanted to wait 'til he got back."

"And he died there," James said flatly.

"I didn't want to be a widow at such a young age. I didn't really mourn long. It just was what it was."

He said, "I'm sorry."

"Survival."

"I'm a survivor, too," he added. "Vietnam. Infantry."

"Excuse me. You don't look like it."

"What should I look like?"

"Wel-l-l…you don't seem uptight. Most of the guys I've seen were screwed up in the head."

He had to pull back. He knew guys like that but didn't consider himself to be one of them. He ordered a Carlsberg from Lianne, who asked, "Would you like another Coke, Aileen?"

"You know, I think I'll have what he's having."

"Aye."

James said, "You don't sound so very Southern."

"That's what I was thinking about you. Where are you really from?"

"Pittsburgh."

With a start, she said, "Pittsburgh! That's where my parents are from."

"Then they must be good people! We have more in common, you and I."

Aileen laughed. "We do indeed."

"So what's your last name, Aileen?"

"Herron. Aileen Caitlin Herron."

James laughed now. "I'm not really Irish. Mostly German, some Dutch, some Welsh."

"How did you get that name?"

"Long ago marriage."

The beers came. They toasted and sipped. She spilled some over her chin and huffed. "Y'know, Mr. Flaherty, I read in *The Post* today that the Travelling Wall is coming to Adare Manor tomorrow."

"What's the Travelling Wall, and what's Adare Manor?"

"It said it was a half-scale replica of the one in Washington. Did you ever go there?"

"Too scared."

"Now's your chance. You'll like Adare Manor. It's so beautiful."

"I….could do that, but I'm not sure it would be good for me."

"I'd think about it. You might be surprised the effect it'll have on you."

"Where is this Adare Manor?"

"The most southern tip of the county. About twelve miles."

"I'm leaving tomorrow afternoon, but I could see it in the morning. I'm ready for a whiskey. Want one?"

"Too dangerous hanging around you. Yes!"

He called Lianne. He ordered the whiskies.

Lianne said, "You too are having a good time. You're turning people's heads."

"That's the way we like it," Aileen said. "Two Americans behaving like Americans!"

Lianne fired back, "Gonna get married, is it?"

James opened his hands. "When are you working tomorrow, Aileen?"

"Afternoon."

"Good. Don't want you to get shitfaced."

"Shitfaced, is it?" Lianne said. "Is that the same as drunk?"

"It is. Only cruder. Remember, we're Americans."

Minutes later with their whiskey. James raised his glass to hers. "Salute!"

"Salute!" she said and tossed it down.

"Careful, Aileen. I don't want to have to carry you to my room."

"Keep dreaming! That's enough for me."

James finished his. "Can you drive home now?"

"Of course. Walk me to the car like the fine Southern gentleman you are."

"Let's go."

Her car was near the back, close to his. He opened the door for her. "Thank you for a wonderful time. And please be careful."

She kissed his cheek before sliding in and said, "Good night, Mr. Flaherty."

* * *

Like a Pittsburgh alley, the car park at Adare Manor was covered by cobblestone and cinder. Standing over buttercups, white cowslip appeared as small hydrangea; of course the ever present roses, and he saw a boxwood topiary above the gate. It depicted a golf ball being addressed by an iron.

"Can I help you?"

He saw that the tall man was missing an arm. "I came to see the Wall."

The tall man focused his dark eyes. "You're American. This sacred ground is for Irish families."

A bit insulted, James replied, "You don't understand. I'm a combat veteran."

"Vietnam, is it?"

"199th, '66 - '67."

The tall man closed in and wrapped his good arm around James and said. "Welcome home, brother. Horace Duane—First Division '65-'66."

James pulled back in surprise. This was the first time he had ever heard that welcome and standing on Irish soil, no less.

"Come with me," Horace said.

James approached a large placard of black canvas, stretching across a slight rise. He asked Mr. Duane if he would take a Polaroid of him standing next to it.

The Wall That Heals: A Traveling Legacy. A half-scale replica of the Vietnam Veterans Memorial in Washington, D.C., has been viewed by nearly eighty million American people in more than eighty American communities and now two countries: the United States and Ireland. — This historic tour of Ireland honors the Irish-born citizens who died while serving with U.S. forces in Vietnam and whose names appear among the 58,214 in this wall, as well as the thousands of Americans of Irish ancestry who also served. This exhibition will help people from Ireland to experience the Wall's healing legacy, which has helped the U.S. to recover from the Vietnam War.

While many walls divide....this wall unites. Dr. David Alderdice, Lord Mayor Belfast.

Horace handed the Polaroid to James, who said, "I think I will treasure this for the rest of my life. I guess I'll look up the names of my fallen comrades."

As he perused the names, a dark cloud came over him. He went through 1966 and 1967. Then he remembered replacements who'd have served in 1968. Slowly scouring, he was shocked to see a ghost from his past: Ardal Shea. The etching smoldered in his mind, and tiny proverbial flames trying to burn it away struck him. The thousand-yard stare returned: a blank gaze into the fog of time. ARDAL SHEA. His closest comrade in the Mekong Delta "wasted." He immediately thought if he had still been there, he might've saved him. They had helped one another throughout the savagery. He saved Ardal from drowning, and Ardal saved him from exhaustive mental collapse. James had always thought his friend had returned to Philadelphia and to his Italian girlfriend. Flaherty backed away, trying to hold back tears. ARDAL SHEA. His friend, his comrade.

"Mr. Flaherty," he heard Horace quietly say. "Have you seen your ghosts?"

"Thank you, brother, and God bless."

* * *

James returned to his car. He sat for a while thinking, '*What am I going to do now?*' he thought. Ardal's family lives in Killorglin, but he had never met them. Maybe the parents were here for the Wall. *Should I just go home and try to forget this, or would it be possible for me to stay on? After all, Horace welcomed me home—on Irish soil! I could go back and see Aileen, but she said she had seen lots of guys with their heads screwed off, and maybe I'm one of them now. Maybe she would help me get through this in a couple days or so. Maybe she'd invite me to her apartment. Just talk. I don't think so.* He started the car and drove to Shannon Airport as he had planned.

There, reliving the shock of his friend's fate, he decided to extend the car rental and cancel his flight home. He drove aimlessly back through Limerick, then turning off roundabouts; he ended up in County Tipperary. He drove south and passed under a rainbow rising above misty rains until he reached Clonmel. It was like a heavenly force driving him now. From Clonmel, he turned east toward…Waterford! He was being taken back to where he began this golf trip, Dunmore East. The Harbor View Inn. The Bohans. 'I can stay there, yes, maybe for a while. I can write a memoir about our time together and deliver it to the Shea's. That's what I'll do. Yes!'

From the outskirts of Waterford City, he came to the factory, where he knew to bear right, go up the hill past the hospital, and on south to Dunmore East. The Harbour View Inn perched on a hill above the sea. Kittiwakes still clamored on the cliffs, and the breeze was gentle now. Holy Cross Catholic Church rested behind on Killea Hill. He saw the fishing wharf below, which was bustling now near the end of the summer day.

To his dismay, the car park was full. He had to find a place on the street, which was also filled. He drove down the hill to find a place at the Haven Hotel. After a ten minute walk back up, in the glow of the sunset, he entered the inn to find Delany Bohan bent over the books. Her curly black hair was sprinkled with silver. She looked up in surprise to find James standing there. "Mr. Flaherty! Forget something?"

"I had to return, Mrs. Bohan. I need a room again for a while."

"Sorry! We're all booked for the summer."

He frowned, deflated, having forgotten the busy summer season had just started. He turned around and through the hallway saw a crowd of men near the end of the bar, and a young woman busily served them drinks. He asked, "Who are they?"

"Welshmen here for the rugby match."

"I can wait for a room 'til they leave."

"Tourists coming in afterward. Booked through most of August."

James sighed. *Maybe I should've stayed in Limerick. But the Woodfield didn't have the quiet I need.* "What about the hotels in town? Surely I can find a place."

"I can call around," she replied, "but I think they're all booked. Tourist season, Mr. Flaherty."

He looked at the young woman pouring a Guinness—attractive, working hard, and her damp face shining.

Delany continued, "Why don't you wait around? You've been here twice, and you're one of our favorites from the States; I'd like to accommodate you."

He motioned to the young woman. "I never saw her before."

"My youngest. She's here from Dingle. Only for a short time before she goes back to her teaching job. Why don't you sit and have a pint while I make some calls?"

The young woman poured and delivered. She stood close, waiting for the Guinness to settle as a pleasant scent followed her. Her hair was thick and wavy, auburn with thin red streaks. He knew her father, Jack, also had red hair. Watching the glass, she finally said, "Now."

He reached and swallowed a first draft. He said, "What's your name?"

She wore a numb face and walked away. He liked that, too. She wore loose jeans and a sweatshirt. He leaned back and slowly slipped. He'd learned to love Guinness. Being from Pittsburgh, where beer reigned, he had an appreciation for the beverage. His attention still honed in on the girl. Maybe she'll tell me her name later, if I get the chance to stay here.

The Welsh men started to get rowdy. They raised their voices higher than their glasses, spitting epithets and sports-lIke cheers. Delaney still worked over her books, the young woman furiously pouring and running, pouring and running.

James thought, I really shouldn't do this. "Can I have some peace and quiet over here?"

"What's the matter, love? Don't like good fun? You could join us, y'know."

James cringed. "Love, is it?"

The young woman finally cracked a smile and acknowledged him.

"Hey!" he called out. "How 'bout a whiskey over here?"

She approached, "You don't have to shout. What can I get ye?"

"A single malt. If you please."

She came back, put the glass on the bar, and winked.

Surprised, James raised his glass. "Thank you."

The Welsh kept picking on one another, as if the match were between their mates.

Delany rose from her work, folded up the books, and came over. "Now, Mr. Flaherty. You said you needed a room for a while. How long?"

"I don't know. Maybe a month or two."

"A…month…or?"

"I was hoping."

"Why, Mr. Flaherty? And so long at the beginning of the season?"

"I don't want to say now. It's too personal."

Delany went to her daughter and said something. The daughter glanced at him, and they whispered, heads together. Delany shook her head.

Her daughter approached. "Mum can't accommodate you, sir. You're going to have to go somewhere else."

"If there's nowhere else, I'm desperate."

"But why so long?" she answered. "Most of our guests stay no longer than a few days. You might wreck our schedule. OK, let us think a bit before I finish and leave."

He liked the sound of her voice and the brogue. He also liked the way she looked—not flashy, but hearty and alive. Her mother waved him to join her outside on the deck, and he followed her out.

Delany said, "I remember you now. You were here for the tournament Jack administered."

"It was a good administration. He was so well organized, and everything went great."

"Tryin' to soften me?"

"Okay, Mrs. Bohan. It's like this,=. I went to see the Vietnam Traveling Wall this morning at Adare Manor. I found out my closest friend got killed over there. He was an Irishman—Ardal Shea. I decided to stay in Ireland to write a memoir for his family."

"Oh my God!. I didn't know you were in Vietnam."

"I don't like to advertise it. I'm looking for some quiet and privacy, and I just thought this would be the best place. The tourists don't bother me, and your family made me feel at home."

Her daughter came out onto the deck. "Mum. They want to see you."

"Not just now, honey. I'm trying to help Mr. Flaherty with his dilemma."

Her daughter stayed with them.

"James," Delany continued, "I'd like to accommodate you. I'm sorry you lost your friend in the war. Let me call around some more, maybe Waterford and Wexford."

"Mum." Her daughter interrupted. "Why not our family sick room? I'm sure Mr. Flaherty could put it to use."

"That might work."

* * *

Delany led her daughter back into the pub, leaving him on the deck. Not sure where he would be sleeping that night, James considered going into the city if necessary; fewer tourists, he reasoned. He could go many places in the country where tourism was not much of a factor, up north, maybe to Mayo or Donegal. Or he could simply return home and do his work from there. But he'd become connected to this place especially after his visit to Adare, when Horace reminded him of it and created the feeling of belonging. Even though he wasn't Irish by descent, his connection to Ireland had been secured by events. At home, his business would interfere. He needed to stay away from it; his reliable assistant ran the place well in his absence. The possibilities presented were all viable. He had plenty of money, had his own transportation, and had the motivation. But the fact was his fallen comrade was Irish. His family lived in Ireland. He'd no doubt been buried in Killorglin.

He thought of his hometown in Pittsburgh. He noticed the remarkable similarities between the two places. The infrastructure's the same: cement steps with iron pipe railings, the brick masonry, the hardwood trees and flowers and bushes, even the weeds were so similar. It boiled down to here or Pittsburgh. He knew how to write; maybe a little rusty, but he might improve as he went along. It was becoming important to him now. No. It had to be here. This was the only option. He just had to hope he could stay with the Bohans. He was tired; he slumped and closed his eyes.

"Okay, Mr. Flaherty," Delany came back outside. "The kids are grown. The need for the sick room's over. We'll give it a try."

He rose and shook her hand. "Thank you so much. I'll gladly pay you for any burden I cause."

"We'll worry about that later. Bernadette will show you the way."

She led him to the second floor and a corner room. The Welsh still frolicked around upstairs, and one even made a pass. "You're a chick, Bernadette, love." She ignored him and opened the door with an old fashioned key. "Here you are."

"That's a huge bed!" James exclaimed. "It takes up all the room."

"You'll find it quite comfortable, Mr. Flaherty."

"Why don't you call me Jimmy?"

"Have you eaten, Mr. Flaherty?"

"Breakfast."

"You'll need something, then."

"Kitchen still open?"

"I can arrange it. Big sister can, but it'll be simple."

"How 'bout just some chips."

"You'll need more than that," she said. "She can do a burger for you."

"That would be nice. Thank you…Bernadette."

"I might be gone when you come downstairs, but Moira will be there."

Jimmy sat on the bed, testing its softness. Charming. He needed to set up. *My bags! They're still in the car, and it's still in the Haven's car park. It's still light; I better go get it now.*

* * *

James slept in. When he awoke in the sick room bed, a gentle breeze ruffled the sheer curtains of the one window in the small room. It would be a sunny day, at least for now. He'd missed breakfast, but he could get something at the Centra up the hill along with writing supplies. Jack and Delany waved to him on the way out. He bought four writing tablets, two pens, two pencils, a ham and cheese sandwich, and an orange. On the way back, he brushed by the iron pipe railing while admiring the harbor. He saw over the western cliff a potato farm with straight green rows sporting white blossoms, and noticed the chestnuts leafing out along the shore. Clover and cowslip flowered near the sidewalk.

At the inn, Jack called out, "Welcome back, Mr. Flaherty."

"Aye," he answered and returned upstairs.

He ate the orange first, then set up his material on the tiny desk. 'Okay, Ardal. I'll do my best, brother. You should be honored by the world, and your family should know what a brave and good soldier you were. James struggled with his memories, long suppressed. It was a chore. He remembered the heat long ago, the canals and muddy rice paddies. The other soldiers who were with them. And the villagers. His company had used the village as a 'hard spot' for both defensive and offensive operations. They went on missions almost every day—helicopter combat assault mostly, but sometimes riverines with the brown-water navy. Then there was the Rung Sat, the mangrove swamp near the sea; dreaded, with strange creatures and stinking mud. All coming back to him: the confusion and terror, the foul smell, the rains, the swift currents.

Uneasy, he decided to go downstairs. Delany poured him a pint of the black stuff. He slowly drank it—thinking. He ordered another and a single malt. How was he going to start this? 'C'mon. Press my thoughts, my memories.

Damn those Americans. They avoided us. They ostracized us. They didn't want to hear the truth. They wanted to keep believing in their follies and didn't want to learn the truth. Typical herd of sheep! Typical educated fools, damn them all to hell! He went back upstairs and tried again to begin.

He lay on the bed still struggling with his memory. 'It shouldn't be that hard. After all, this is Ardal. We were brothers. We were each other's saviors.' He decided to go back to the bar. This time, it was Bernadette. "Single malt and Smithwick's." He drank quickly. Another whiskey and a Guinness.

She accommodated two more rounds but finally said, "No more."

He slurred as he stepped off the stool, knees buckling, "Why don't you come up to my room? We can have a good time."

"MISTER FLAHERTY! You're drunk. You need to go to your room alone!"

"I don't think I can stand."

"Then I'll help ye."

"Let your father help me."

"He's not here. He and Mum went home."

She came around the bar and tightly locked his arm, lifting him. She was surprisingly strong. She pulled him up the stairs and into his room then left him swaying next to the bed. "Don't let me have to undress ye. Go to sleep."

Another late start the next morning, he had only a slight headache, as he'd been used to heavy drinking since coming back from the war. Remembering his embarrassment last night, he walked down the stairs and sat on the deck, and knew now he had to control himself and get on with his self-appointed task. His head cleared enough for deep thinking and stared out toward the harbor and cliffs, but didn't smell the salt air or see the fishing boats there, as horrid memories floated back. He now knew the best way to start would be when he met Ardal for the first time. From there, the story would flow; his memory would follow. He rose from the chair and returned to his room: time to begin.

I first met Ardal in February 1967. He came to u —Company B, Second Battalion, Third Infantry, 199th Light Infantry Brigade — with crisp new fatigues, shiny boots, and a brand new M-16. I said, "Hi. James Flaherty."

"Ardal Shea," he replied.

"You have an accent."

"Irish, I'm from Ireland."

"Cool. I never met an Irishman before, but tell me, why the hell are you here?"

"Volunteered."

Stunned, I said, "Here?!"

"A quick path to citizenship," he replied.

I studied the new guy. Muscular, medium height, he had black hair and brown eyes.

His face presented a seriousness and determination, a contradiction to the fear we all had. But I knew that would change. Once tested, he'd come around to us, a part of the Green Machine.

Ardal looked out over the village, "I thought there'd be more lads here."

"We started with two hundred men. Now we have fewer than a hundred. This is Vietnam, Shea. Casualties, disease, heat stroke, and swamp foot have whittled us down. With some more replacements like you, maybe we'll get to a hundred and fifty. Have you met Lieutenant Sam yet?"

"Not yet."

"He's our platoon leader. Let's find him."

Each platoon had a large tent raised for sleeping quarters. They found Sam sitting in front of it. "Lieutenant, this is Ardal Shea."

"Great, Company CP sent you. Captain Turner told me a replacement was on the way. Welcome."

"Sorry, sir," I answered, "I intercepted him before he got to you."

"Fine. Flaherty, I'm assigning him to you. Understand?"

"And Shea," he added, "listen very carefully. James is seasoned, and he might save your life. Settle in. We have a mission tomorrow. Company; AO Brenda."

James led Ardal to the weapon-cleaning station near the river. "Let me inspect your M-16. Looks good. Clean it yet?"

"No."

"You'll need to oil it. Tropical weather requires more lubrication than normal. Your grenades. Where would you carry them?"

"On my belt, naturally."

"Nope, wrong answer. We cross many canals and rivers. Always carry your grenades on your shoulder straps, and two only. You don't want to get weighed down in this mud. No pack. One canteen. Salt pills. Iodine pills. As many bandoliers as you can carry."

Ardal looked confused "That's not what they told us in training."

[sigh] "Training is for conventional warfare. Here we deal with Charlie, man, child, or woman, who will have no hesitation to waste your ass."

"Okay. I'll follow your orders."

"Advice, Shea. We'll all be giving you valuable advice. If you survive, we survive. That's what it's all about. Can you swim?"

"Yes."

"Strong?"

"Strong."

"Good. We've lost some guys who didn't know how to swim. Valuable skill. Get your shit together, and we'll be ready for tomorrow."

* * *

We stood on the dirt road north of the village of Phu Le. "Nervous?" I asked Ardal.

"First time out. I'm scared."

"We're all scared. You'll get used to it."

"Smoke out! Color yellow!" called Captain Turner.

The choppers came in a straight line, lifted their noses, and settled on the road. We climbed in and felt the birds' slow lift off. They flew in unison, just skimming the highest branches near tree top level. Arriving at Brenda, we banked and lowered to just above soft ground. Since they couldn't land in the mud, we had to jump. I pulled Ardal out behind me, and we both landed knee deep. As the ships left for the second lift, we spread into a line. Lt. Sam radioed Company, "Cold LZ."

We waited for the next two lifts, keeping close vigilance for signs of enemy activity. We sucked our feet out of the mud. "I didn't expect this," Ardal said. "I thought it was all jungle."

"Welcome to the Mekong Delta," Sam said. "The worst AO in the entire country."

The second lift came in. Reinforced, we spread out in a line with weapons at the ready. Suddenly, we heard the crack thump from a distant tree line. **CRACK THUMP, CRACK THUMP!** The third lift arrived. We all moved toward the tree line and fired back, taking return fire. One soldier was shot in the arm inside his elbow.

The captain radioed to see if the wounded man needed a dust-off. A sergeant answered "yes!" Firing from the trees continued, including a machine gun. Now we returned fire, using every weapon we had. I saw Ardal firing his M-16 on full automatic.

We paused firing when the medivac arrived, followed by two gunships. Three soldiers helped the wounded man into the rescue helicopter as gunships prowled around the area.

"One-six, two-six, three-six," the captain called on the radio.

"This is one-six, over."

"This two-six, over."

"This is three-six over."

Six was the designation for leaders. "This is six; get ready to move out. Two more clicks." [Kilometers]

Ardal and I sat on a berm. "Shea," I said. "You don't have to fire auto. It's not accurate except in close combat. Better to fire well-aimed single shots."

The call to move came over the horn [radio]. We rose to get back on line. The second tree line we penetrated with ease. Moving forward, we came close to a third group of trees, thick with hedges, shaped into a semi-circle. Turner ordered a halt, and we received heavy fire immediately — machine guns and small arms. Our artillery came crashing into the hedges followed by airbursts. None of us was hit. Turner told us to set up chalks into a pickup zone, as the smoke lifted and we gathered ourselves.

"Our captain has an uncanny sense about the VC," I grinned to Ardal. "They were leading us into a battalion-size ambush."

We arrived back at the village an hour later. After returning to our Platoon area, Lt .Sam asked Ardal, "What do you think about our mission?"

"Scary."

"Be prepared. We do this every day. Now clean up your weapon and get ready for ambush or guard."

"Ambush?"

"We send out ambushes every night."

His eyes strained, and Flaherty decided to go to the bar for a break. There he saw Miss Bohan sitting on a stool inside the far corner. "May I have a Guinness?"

"You look knackered."

"Working hard. Memories haunting."

She set the pint down, and after the foam had properly settled, she said, "Now."

"I'm a Trinner," she added.

"What's that?"

"I graduated from Trinity College in Dublin."

"What did you study?"

"Languages. I admire what you're doing, Mr. Flaherty. Mum told me. Maybe I could help? I could edit your memoir."

"Too personal, but thanks anyway."

Halfway through the pint, "Miss Bohan, where could I find some relaxation in this 'ville? I need to get away from my desk for a while. Change of venue, you might say."

"We do have a disco up the street at Slaney's."

"I love to dance; been doin' it since I was a teenager."

"So, after we close, I usually go there to see my friends. If I were you, I'd suggest going up there about eleven."

"Thanks, Miss Bohan. I can throw down tonight!"

She tightened her lips. "Throw down, is it?"

Around ten James came down the stairs to see Miss Bohan sitting on her familiar stool in the now quiet lounge.

"Ready?" she smiled.

"Did we just make a date?"

"Of course not, Mr. Flaherty! I just want to introduce you to my friends. Straightaway."

Out on the sidewalk, he noticed the blue plaid skirt and her tan boots. She wore a white blouse and a light blue baseball cap.

"You're well dressed," he told her. Her hazel eyes reflecting lights from the nearby shops, she stepped lightly, as James remembered himself almost bouncing across the fairways of Lahinch. He walked on the outside of the sidewalk and offered his arm, which she ignored. "I'm going on the tear tonight." She winked at him.

What the hell is that? he thought. He opened the door for her and followed her into the loud, smoke-filled bar, where they were surrounded by her friends, and hugs and cheek-kissing. "So," said a blonde. "Who is this fine thing, Bernadette?"

"This is Mr. Flaherty. He's staying at the inn for a few weeks." To James, "This is my dear friend, Caroline."

"Hello, Caroline. Should we hug or shake hands?"

"Whichever."

"Why don't you two dance?" Miss Bohan offered.

"Hey! Excuse me! I see someone I know over there. He was our caddy for the tournament." Getting through the crowd, he rounded the horseshoe bar to the makeshift stage, "Aidan!"

"Jim!" What are you doing here?"

"That's what I was going to ask you. How did the football trials go in London?"

"Pretty well, but I didn't make it."

"Tough, I know how much it meant to you."

"Yuh, I have to work here to repay my parents. I have a day job, as well."

"That's quite a collection of music there. I wonder if you would do me a favor? I'm here with Bernadette Bohan."

"She's wonderful. Ye know she's a Trinner."

"She told me."

"Where did you meet her? And how did you get so lucky to date her?"

"We're not on a date. I'm staying at the inn for a while, which leads me to the favor. Could you play a song at the end: This Magic Moment?"

"I don't know. I'll have to check if I have it here." He pointed to his vast collection.

"Thanks, Aidan. I'll see you around."

James went back to the bar where he had left the girls. They were gone, but there was a young man. "Where did Bernadette and Caroline go?"

"They're out on the dance floor. You must be James Flaherty."

"How did you know?"

"I'm Ollie." He extended his hand.

James returned the shake. Ollie had short-cut red hair and a thin beard.

"How do you know my name?"

"She's been talking about you."

"Good or bad?"

"Good."

"How do you know her?"

"Same schools, but different church. It's obvious she likes you. I like her, too. I always have. She's cute, smart, and a lot of fun. I'd really like to see her more often."

"Why don't you come visit her at the inn?"

"Mr. Flaherty, what's your first name?"

"James. But you can call me Jimmy."

Just then Caroline showed up. "C'mon James Flaherty, dance with me."

Most of the music came from the fifties and later. Caroline and James danced well together in the steps and movements that went with it. A curly-haired girl joined them. "You dance well!" she yelled over the music.

"What's your name?"

"I'm Bernadette's friend, Harper."

"Nice hair."

"Yours, too! I'm breaking in."

Aidan played "The Twist," bringing the house down. Harper moved with it perfectly, and James worked hard to keep up with her.

"You're good!" he yelled.

Harper winked and smiled.

After six pints and two whiskeys, he began to feel the fog of the evening. Everybody danced to the oldies, including the guys and Caroline and Bernadette. When Aiden played The Supremes, they sang along. Then came The Wanderer, when those on the crowded dance floor raised their glasses. Credence continued the revelry, and Motown. During a break, the girls were having tequila shots with a ravishing redhead who had joined them. They rose when hearing Janis Joplin belt out "hoo-hoo-wa."

When Aidan played "Sweet Caroline,'" men started to close in, but James got to Caroline before them. He took her onto the floor, and they danced in unison, as she swayed her arms and sang along. Song over, Bernadette led over her red-haired friend. "This is Ellsbeth, another dear friend of mine."

"Pleasure."

The dancing had slowed. Most people sat in groups to visit and drink, and gossiping, too, James imagined. His group was the four girls and Ollie. Caroline said, "You really know how to dance, James."

"Jimmy. Call me Jimmy. Y'all dance well, too." He raised his new pint and toasted. They fell into whispering small talk, and he could hear other conversations nearby. The night almost over, Bernadette leaned over and slurred, "Did…you…have Mighty Craic?"

The girls were gathering their purses and wraps, buzzing about where they'd see each other again, when Aidan came through with "Magic Moment." They paused and watched as James gently led Bernadette to the floor and encircled her waist. She awkwardly pushed him to a distance. As the song went on, her head leaned side to side, and when she tried to raise it, her eyes closed. *Damn,* James thought, *she's drunk. I thought Irish girls could hold their liquor.*

She stumbled forward into his chest, her head resting there. He raised her chin at the verse, "When your lips are close to mine, it will last forever, til the end of time." He held her by the elbow as they left the floor. "Me thinks she needs some help getting home."

"I'll help." It was Ollie.

"Oh, no thanks, I can get home!" She looked at James and said, "C'mon."

Outside, she leaned against James and walked well at first, then began to stagger. "I shouldn't have had that tequila," she muttered and hiccupped.

James added, "You could hallucinate from that stuff, too. Hold on."

"Mr. Flaherty, I don't think I can make it home. We'll have to go to the inn."

"And sleep where? The inn is full!"

"The sick room," she said.

James then slumped. *This is bad. I'll get into big trouble. I can't afford this, but what else can I do?* They reached the inn where he helped her stumble up the stairs. *The other girls seemed fine. Maybe Bernadette isn't accustomed to drinking.* He opened the door and eased her onto the bed then covered her with a blanket. Fortunately, his writing chair was cushioned, and he used a quilt to wrap around himself in the chair. She snored. Waking in the darkness several times, he finally dozed into uncomfortable sleep.

As daylight crept through the window, James sat awake in the chair.

Bernadette stirred, rolled up, looked around, and saw James. "O Mo Dia! I'm so embarrassed." Her cheeks reddened. "I'm so ashamed! Forgive me, Mr. Flaherty."

"Jimmy."

"James." She held her head in her hands and yawned.

"Going home now?"

She groaned and stretched. "I can't. I'll go over to Caroline's for some talk and brown bread."

"You mean gossip. I'm going to sleep."

"Magic Moment." She yawned again, got up painfully, and left.

mekong delta

Shea and I sat together on post for the village guard. Before dusk, we had a wide view around us. Hard clay ground provided a place for our air mattresses.

"Do you know any of these villagers?" Ardal asked.

"A few, especially the barber."

"The village has a barber?"

"A good one, too."

Across the paddies the heat still rose in waves, and thatched houses in the distance seemed to float like corks on a sea of green grass. Just before dark, Lieutenant Sam came inspecting the post. "Ardal, how do you feel after your first mission?"

"Honestly, a little edgy."

Sam said, "You'll get used to it."

"With James' help."

"That's what I like to hear. We're going on a platoon mission tomorrow. Lookin' for bodies. Be vigilant tonight. I'll see you guys in the morning."

I could see Ardal thinking. "Do we go on missions every day?"

"Sweeps. Yes, almost every day. Sometimes we go on riverines with the brown water navy."

"That sounds interesting."

I said, "Two hour shifts. I'll take the first." Two hours later, still quiet, I nudged him awake and settled on my mattress, my head on my helmet. I fell into a deep slumber.

I dreamt I was in my old neighborhood in Pittsburgh. *We teenagers got into fights. I wasn't good at it, so I used diplomacy for evading. We had some tough guys always picking for a fight: George Canan—almost a midget—was the worst. He finally made his fame by breaking into the Post Office. Then there was Mary McKittrick, the most feared among us. She made it a sport beating up on guys. She always won. I avoided her by telling her how pretty she was, which she wasn't.*

In the dream, I was in the breakfast joint out on the Twin Highways. I was eating potatoes. And then I was with a girl, and she pulled me into an alley. She unzipped my pants and pulled me to her. She put her fingers on my massive boner. I dreamed I was about to enter her…

"James! What's that?" Ardal pointed to the big river far downstream. A light observation helicopter danced around like a giant stinging insect, and a candlelight flare revealed a circling gunship. They spotted a target as the gunship fired rockets.

"You woke me up for that?!" I shook my head.

"It scared me."

"It's just a hunter-killer team."

"Sorry."

"I was about to have a great wet dream."

"Oh, I'm really sorry, man."

"You didn't know." Thinking about the lost wet dream, I said, "Hey. Did you ever get jacked off by an Irish girl?"

"We call it a handshake. Once."

"Was she pretty?"

"Blonde."

"Was it good?"

"I was fluthered."

"What's that?"

"Too many drinks at my uncle's pub. The girl I was with helped me home."

"That's when she jerked—gave you a handshake?"

"It wasn't any good."

* * *

A platoon mission only required six helicopters. We set up six chalks with six men each for the loading. The morning was already warming as the birds flew high at first, gunships circling us. As we descended, we peered out the side doors before jumping onto the landing zone. Lieutenant Sam radioed company CP - "Cold LZ."

"Be careful," Captain Turner barked.

"Wilco, out."

We formed up and went on line, moving to a heading of 120 degrees [southeast]. Now hot, with a blazing sun, the soft mud made progress more difficult. Sergeant McKenzie stepped in over his knees, then Lorenzo went down to his waist. It took two of us to pull him free, cursing and straining. We entered a tree line with deep ditches guarded by palms, and we found blood trails here and there, but no bodies. "We probably won't find bodies," I told Shea. "The VC doesn't leave them behind. Our body count is measured by blood trails."

"You mean the trails count as bodies?"

"That's how McNamara sees it."

"Who's McNamara?"

"Our Secretary of Defense. He's all about the numbers."

We continued our march through the trees. We saw more trails on the next paddy and were tracking them forward when a single rifle shot cracked past us If we could hear the crack-thump, none of us got hit.

"Carbine!" I cried out.

Immediately we returned fire. Rickie-Bear held his M60 Machine gun waist high and shot mud geysers spurting up from the ground; we saw the rounds traverse a dike. More carbine fire: pop! crack! pop!.

"Get down, Ardal!"

We joined the machine gun and fired M16's furiously. The carbines stopped. We charged, crouched, running over rice stalks and mud. Behind the berm lay four dead, one woman and three men, on the muddy ground. A rare occasion to see the results of our craft. Ardal stared at the dead, flies already landing. "What are we going to do with these bodies?"

"Leave them for the crabs!" Rickie-Bear growled.

Lieutenant Sam said, "Four more. Let's add them to our count. Spread out."

He got on the horn. "Six, this is three-six, over."

"This is six, over."

"Three-six. Mission complete."

"Roger. Need PZ?"

"That's a rog on that."

Thirty minutes later we heard the helicopters coming. The birds banked around the trees for a soft landing. We closed and climbed into the choppers through the diesel exhaust. On the way back, we lifted high into the sky as two gunships ran shotgun.

Walking into the village, we felt the electricity from the mission. Second time out, and Ardal came under fire again and saw dead bodies. We came together at the platoon tent near the river. Shea was quiet for a while, then said, "Now I know it's real."

Lieutenant Sam returned from CP. "Okay. Listen up. We're going on a company trip to AO Liza. Two and a half clicks."

"Liza?" said Lee. "That's as far as we go."

Ardal asked, "What's Liza all about?"

"Hardcore Indian country," I replied. "Those people are psychotic. VC propaganda makes them crazy."

"That bad?"

"You can be sure we're going to get hit. And hard."

James saw Delany at the bar. "Good morning, ma'am."

"Slept late, did ya, Jimmy? Enjoy disco?"

"Much."

"I heard you're a good dancer."

"Ever since high school."

"Do you think Bernadette would like to go into the city with me?"

"You'd have to ask her. She has to tend bar this afternoon."

"Not enough time. Maybe tomorrow."

The next morning, they set out for Waterford City Center, Bernadette driving her car. She was to do some shopping, and James wanted to see the town. Passing schools and a park, he enjoyed her smooth maneuvering around the traffic circles.

She downshifted for the curve past the hospital and found parking in a roofless garage. She looked up, gathering her purse. "I have to hit the jacks before shopping. Shall we meet back here in about two hours?"

"Sure."

"See ya then."

She returned carrying a large box and a small shopping bag. James had a small paper bag of postcards.

"It's time for lunch." Bernadette said. "Do you like Chinese?"

"Sounds great."

"We can walk." She hooked her arm around his elbow.

The restaurant smelled of joss, and the decor was plastic lanterns and terra cotta figureheads of dragons and tigers. They were led to a small table next to the window facing the street. Menus and napkins quickly followed. A thin waiter arrived; Bernadette asked for oolong tea, and James ordered jasmine.

After looking over the menu, she asked, "What's your chancer?"

"Everything spicy."

"If it's not too bold, how old are you?"

"Thirty-eight."

Her jaw dropped. "You don't even look close to that! I'm curious about your writing about Vietnam. You mind if I read some?"

James leaned back and felt the soft cushion of his chair. He had to think about that.

"I'd rather not. It's too personal."

"How am I going to get to know you?"

The waiter was back.

"I'll have cashew shrimp and scallops," she said.

"I would like chicken kung pao."

Upon finishing he asked, "Would you like some lychee for dessert?"

"What's that?"

"An Asian fruit. Give it a try; I used to have it in Vietnam."

After finishing lunch there, they walked back to the car park

"Ready to load the cart and go home?"

Leaving the bustle of Waterford, she drove toward Dunmore East, where James saw purple spiderwort spread wildly in the fields and under fence posts. Farm gardens grew red, white, and yellow roses in clusters. Purple and white iris bared their throats around doors and windows, while golden chrysanthemum fluttered in the afternoon breeze. She down-shifted, fourth to third to second as she pulled into the driveway before her house. "I'll take my shopping in and we'll walk to the inn, if that's alright." She came back outside, and they started toward the inn.

"Are you working tonight?"

"Oh, yes, while I'm here, every night. But before I start, I'd like to sit with you and talk some more."

Along the way they smelled freshly cut grass among the small gardens. Bernadette's face glowed beneath her bangs. Arriving at the inn, they met Moira, sitting at the bar. "Bernadette. How was your trip to town? Did you and Mr. Flaherty have any fun?"

"We ate Chinese. Mr. Flaherty introduced me to lychee."

"What's that?"

"Asian fruit. Delicious."

Moira winked. "Can you relieve me about an hour or so?"

"Sure, in a bit."

The couple went into the den. She sat close to James. Her pink cheeks reflected the glow of the peat fire. "Thanks for the good time, Mr. Flaherty. May I ask you more about Vietnam?"

"It's hard enough to write about it, but okay."

"Did you ever come close to death?"

"Several times."

Delany appeared from around the corner. "Here, James. A fresh pint and a single malt. On the house." She set the glasses down.

He looked up. "Oh, thanks, Mrs. Bohan."

"Like I was saying, several times. The last time was especially harrowing."

"Tell me about it."

"Sure?"

"Very sure."

"Alright, then, I was working for the information office in Can Tho. The editor was a Navy lieutenant who heard from this air cav commander complaining about how little recognition his men got. He told our editor he was worried about his men's morale. The editor called me into his office and told me I was the only one on the staff with combat experience. He wanted to put me on the story, but only if I volunteered."

"And you did," Bernadette said. She leaned closer.

"I knew how important morale was to a combat unit, so I did." He could smell her fresh hair.

"We drove out to the cav's base camp, where I boarded a command and control chopper. Then we went flying over a place called the U Minh Forest, a very dangerous area the Vietnamese call the 'place of the big mosquitoes.' .' Circling high overhead, we watched a South Vietnamese Division attack a NVA bunker—the cavalry throwing grenades into the bunkers and firing their machine guns."

"Then a triangle of anti-aircraft weapons fired at the ship. The tracers zipped through us, and our pilot took us high above the clouds, and it was cold up there, and then he flew some distance before going into autorotation."

"What's that?"

"When the ship loses its power, the pilot has to use updraft to land it: go down and pull up, go down and pull up using the prop wash to ease the landing." She saw beads of sweat on his forehead. His fingers trembled. "Anyway, we made it back to the landing strip. We found bullet holes in the bottom, stitched the length of the helicopter, and realized how lucky we were. The pilot said if he hadn't taken the bird so high, it might have exploded."

"Incredible," Bernadette said. "You really are a warrior."

"More importantly, I'm a survivor." Elbows on his thighs, he lowered his head into his hands and sobbed.

Bernadette touched his arm and sighed. "I'm so sorry."

"What you don't understand is the guilt."

"Why should you feel guilty?"

"Because I made it and others didn't."

"Like Ardal?"

"And many others. Why did I live and they didn't?"

He straightened up and stared into the fireplace.

She looked at him. "I'll leave you alone to think."

"No! I need you here. Let's change the subject."

Bernadette was lost for words; her look was questioning.

He said, "I've decided to let you read my memoir."

"I consider that to be an honor. May I edit for you?"

"Please do. I want it to be as perfect as possible."

She placed her hand on his. "I'll make it so. Now I know why you enjoy your drink; you are a Celtic warrior."

"So. When are you going back to Dingle?"

"When I finish helping here at the inn."

"When is that?"

"When school goes back to session in September."

"Do you like Dingle?"

"Very much. It's wild, like you."

"Oh, yeah, like me," He winked.

Fifteen helicopters lined the dirt road. Unusual for a sweep mission, they stretched almost to the next village. Captain Turner ordered each platoon leader to assign four men for mud-pulling duty; he didn't want easy targets. Our whole company would land in the hot LZ together.

The prop wash bent the new rice stalks almost to the mud. Our uniforms flapped until we boarded. Each soldier prayed. Wide-eyed, Ardal shook my hand and locked and loaded his M-16.

The birds separated into two groups. Six gunships, with miniguns and rockets, circled like eagles. As we descended, the door gunners opened up, aiming for the tree lines. The gunships fired rockets. As we jumped out, sure enough, some men got stuck in knee-deep mud; Ardal was one of them. I wasn't assigned as a mud-puller, but I rushed to him and hauled him out. Automatic and rifle fire flared at us. We ferociously fired back, as if we wanted an end to the savage Liza.

Ardal and I and others spread to the left flank where we continued to lay out suppressive fire until we were able to get on line. The hostiles fell silent. We pushed on, sometimes sinking into the mud, and approached a wide river. From the village on the other side, we heard the familiar thumping of mortars.

"Sixties!" someone screamed. The rounds sizzled in, loud and frightening, and our men started falling everywhere. We heard screams. We felt the earth rumble, and we smelled the black powder. Medics scrambled to the wounded, still screaming.

I looked at Shea. "I hate this place. I hate Liza!"

Gunships lined up to attack the village, but were reluctant to fire on innocents. Our 79 gunners moved closer to the river. They honed in on bunkers and fired. One ship got hit and began to smoke; the pilot brought it in with a soft landing, and he and the crew chief gathered behind our line. The pilot was armed with only a .45 pistol; the crew chief with an M-16. We had to protect them as best we could.

Into the smoke and chaos, medivacs floated like butterflies to pick up the strewn bodies of the dead and wounded. The mortar fire stopped, but automatic and small arms fire continued from the village. Ardal and I fired on full auto until our magazines ran low; then we fired single shots. Under such repressive fire, the enemy's' weapons finally fell silent.

Only ten choppers were now needed for pickup. We raced toward them and dove in. Shea slid across the floorboard, but we caught him before he planned out the other side. Small arms fire unleashed again as the helicopters rose. We lifted off with great speed, and quickly climbed high. The Delta wind hit us through the open doors, and we bunched up close together against the chill. The blades started chopping in the wind, and we finally made it back to the village and piled out, limping and muddy. Somberly, we went to our platoon tents. Ardal and I sat on the sandbags outside our tent.

Some of the men cried and vomited, repeating, "Wasted!"

I complained, "I don't know why they keep sending us there. That place can never be pacified."

"Why do we bother, then?"

"The other two companies go there, too. I have a friend in C Company who got drafted the same day as I did, and trained together, who told me about this lieutenant that he RTO'd for, who attacked two bunkers and wiped them out. And for what?"

"Good question, James."

"I guess."

"You know," Ardal then said, "What struck me was how long we were fightin.' It seemed like hours but lasted no more than fifteen, twenty minutes. Talk about compressed time."

"It's always like that. I don't know. Maybe adrenaline."

Lieutenant Sam came for his usual rounds. He stepped before us, fists clenched, and said, "Do you fellas know what my real name is?"

After blank stares, he piped, "Simon! I hate that name! Always hated it."

"Why are you telling us?" I asked.

"Because I hate this place worse!"

"We do, too!"

"Not as much as I do. It's worthless. I get tired of wasting soldiers for Vietnam, The Republic Of." He shook his head. He paused, then added, "You're going out on bush tonight, so be prepared; I'd hate to lose you two."

Ardal asked, "What was the casualty count?"

"Were. What were the casualty count. 16 K's, 22 wounded. Wasted."

Ardal and I didn't appreciate the grammar lesson. It didn't seem correct, anyway.

"That's just wonderful." I sighed. "Until we get more replacements, we're badly under strength. What the fuck, over!"

* * *

For the night's ambush, eight of us commandeered two sampans to ferry us the quarter-mile up river. The papasans were reluctant and visibly worried. "They know the danger," McKenzie said. "Just look at 'em."

We disembarked to a position that presented us with a three-way view. A canal split right off the small river, eclipsing a large paddy. We set up a line. Our weapons locked and loaded, we spread out our bedding and waited for darkness.

"I love the sunset in the tropics," Lee said in a whisper, "Look at that orange sky. At least there's one good thing here."

McKenzie, all business, said, "One or two?"

"Let's do two," I offered. "This place gives me the creeps."

"Okay, then. James, you and Ardal take the second shift. Lorenzo and Metger take the first. Lee and Peter, then me and Willie there. Let's sleep. Wake me if you see or hear anything."

As darkness fell, CP did the thirty minute commo check. "Two, three, this is six oscar, how hear?" from a low voice.

Lorenzo pushed the squelch two times. "Roger," the voice whispered back in the quiet.

The check would be at two hour intervals throughout the night.

Darkness enveloped us. There were no lights from the villages, and the sounds fell silent. Eerie. Ardal and I were nudged awake by Lorenzo. He handed me the radio handset, then quickly went to sleep. The day's action exhausted us. Ardal, on edge, set into hypervigilance. Hard to stay awake, we rubbed our eyes and silently yawned. Late in the dry season, the Delta wind came; breezy at first, then windy. Eventually, we wrapped our ponchos around us and crouched lower. Suddenly, we heard slurping nearby. We couldn't see in the darkness, but definitely heard the noise. Slurp...slurp...slurp. Slow and measured. Slurp...slurp. Footsteps. I nudged McKenzie and whispered, "There's people behind us."

"How many?"

"I can't tell yet. Keep listening."

McKenzie nudged everybody down the line with his finger on his lips. "Enemy."

The slurping stopped. We trained our weapons, hearts pounding. Strained our ears. Seconds turned to minutes; minutes to hours. Breathless now, we braced for explosive energy. I thought I saw one. I aimed and fired; no response. I fired again, and then we all did; Tracers bounced skyward; seventy-nine explosions thumped. Still no return. More blasts, and then return fire began zipping past us with horrifying snaps.

"Ow!" Peter cried."

Just as suddenly as it started, it stopped. The enemy seemed to melt away.

Peter moaned and whimpered while Ardal opened the soldier's first aid kit, pulled out a large bandage, and pressed it to Peter's bleeding shoulder. We hovered around the wounded man to wait for dawn.

The radio crackled with loud, alarmed voices. "Two, three, two, three, you hit?"

"Roger. One man down. Need dust-off."

The rest of our platoon appeared from the rear, tracing the path, looking for the enemy. But they were gone.

Back to our platoon CP at daybreak, we praised and hugged Shea. "You saved Peter! We love you, Ardal."

I put my arms around him and kissed his cheek.

"Thank you."

At 6:00 a.m. in the dining room, James found himself picking at his food. What he'd just written severely depressed him; he hadn't slept well. While having coffee, he perused the Waterford News and Star. "Mr. Flaherty," Jack came close to the table. "You look tired."

"Yuh, a bit crestfallen."

"Why don't you take a break? A day off. I can make an appointment at Faithlegg."

"I'd like that, Mr. Bohan."

"Say about ten?"

"Ten, then. Perfect."

Later that morning James brought his clubs and golf shoes down to the small foyer. He moved outside to the deck and sat on one of the lounge chairs. He watched young mothers pushing strollers up and down the street. They wore their traditional thick black stockings and shawls to keep warm. The little ones were draped like papooses in the morning air.

Only two months and she'll be gone. Can't get her out of my head. I like her. Everything.

James remembered the church doctrine that sex is blessed for procreation only. He had been a good Catholic until he reached the age of reason. He believed in the pleasure between a man and a woman. He wondered if she were a good Catholic. He wondered how it would feel being with her, but he knew it would never happen; he would be back in the States, and she would go back to Dingle in two months. He went back inside.

"Well, James, ready?"

"Yes sir."

They took the highway toward town for a few miles then turned right onto an old dirt road to the course.

"Bring your clubs and shoes with you."

"Shane, this is my American friend who's boarding with us. James Flaherty, this is Shane Rogin."

"Where in the States?"

"South Carolina."

"Great golfing. The four of us are planning to holiday there. May I talk with you when you come in?"

"Sure."

All they saw ahead was a threesome on the second fairway. James and Jack hit good shots on the short par four first hole. They hit wedges to the green for pars. On the second tee, they made their way for bogies on the par five. When they reached the par three third hole, the threesome had yet to putt. James said, "Why don't we wait until they putt out and hit from the next tee?"

"There's nobody behind us," Jack said. He rested his fist on his chin and leaned on his six iron. He had a barrel chest over a stout, shortish body. "May I ask you a personal question?"

"Depending on what it is."

"What was it like being a soldier in Vietnam?"

"Uh-h-h."

"You don't have to answer."

"I can put it in a single word—terrifying."

Jack mulled. He looked out to the next green and rubbed his nose. "Does it bring back bad memories?"

"Too many."

"Sorry to intrude. I'll never mention it again."

"Between us, Mr. Bohan, I've broken and cried at times."

"Sorry."

"Save it for my next bad shot."

When the threesome cleared the next tee, both men hit; Jack to the right side, James with his high shot on the green. Walking to the green, Jack said, "I notice you like to hit high shots,"

"It fits our climate better."

He shook his head. "Just like Bernadette plays."

"She plays?"

"Ever since she was fourteen."

"That's the same age when I started."

"Yuh. My daughter's quite the athlete. Do you know her mother is a three time champion at Dunmore East Club?"

"Does all your family play?"

"Lad. This is Ireland."

Jack chipped ten feet and passed the flag; James two-putted for a par. Jack made his ten-footer. The next hole was a 330 yard par-four downhill with the fairway slanting slightly to the right. James had honors. He teed up and stepped back.

"By the way, Mr. Bohan, I've grown fond of your daughter."

"How much?" James took out his three-wood and hit a draw against the slope. "Nice shot. Are you becoming close to Bernadette?"

"In a friendly way. Aside from being attractive, she's smart and a good conversationalist. She doesn't realize it, but I'm learning some Irish vernacular through her."

Jack hit his driver to the right. The ball settled near the grass lining the fairway. James walked over with him; he could smell the cocoanut scent from the blossoms. "Maybe you should've hit a four wood."

Jack grumbled. He lined up his shot. "You think I have a good enough back swing?"

"Looks like it. Take some practices."

James returned to his ball and took out an eight iron. He drew his ball close to the pin; it looked like birdie, he thought. Jack dubbed. It went rolling along the ground, but close to the green. "Feck!" He threw his club.

James made it a point to avoid him until he regained his composure. Stereotypical red head, he supposed. Jack recovered with a chip onto the green. James tapped in his birdie. They quietly played on and finished out with Jack at fourteen points and James at twelve. "Mr. Bohan, why is Bernadette not married? She looks to be in her twenties."

"Twenty six come this July; she'll be twenty seven. July fourteen, to be exact."

"Bastille day."

"That's why we named her Bernadette." He took off his Kangol hat and stroked his head. "You see, James, those years in Dublin changed her. She got used to big city life and just couldn't readjust to a small village like Dunmore East."

"But Dingle is not exactly a metropolis."

"Yuh. But her mind is occupied there. Do you know she has a fella?"

"Oh? Good for her; especially him."

"We've only met the man once. They work together in intermediate school."

"What's intermediate school?"

"I believe you call it high school."

"What does she teach?"

"English. People in Dingle speak Gaelic, so she teaches them English."

"What does her fella teach?"

"I don't know yet. Let's hit before it gets dark."

It didn't seem close to dusk to James. The back nine was more open and much windier. Both of them hit their drivers onto the par-five fairway. With the shorter tee shot, James decided to lay up with a four iron. Mr. Bohan hit his four-wood almost to the green. Jack birdied, and James bogeyed.

Tit for tat, they continued to the River Suir and back around. They finished on the difficult par-four eighteen; took off their hats and shook hands. "I enjoyed our time. Thanks, Mr. Flaherty."

In the clubhouse, James admired the exposed oak ceiling beams, the large fireplace, and the angled bar. Jack came from the bar holding two pints; he a Bulmer's hard cider; James a Guinness. Shane followed with a whiskey. "I know you like whiskey with your beer," Jack said. The three sat down around the small table. "So Mr. Flaherty, a group of us plan a golfing holiday to South Carolina. What would you recommend?"

"There are no links courses on the Grand Strand. If you can go anywhere in the state, I'd recommend the Midlands. They have many fine courses there, and they're not crowded like the beach. My home course, Linrick, has a fine layout, and it's well kept. What time of year are you planning?"

"We're thinking Autumn."

"Perfect," James said. "The weather should be in the 70s or 80s.

"I'll pass that on, James. Thanks."

"So what about you?" Jack said. What's your situation? Finances, I mean."

Wondering why he had asked such a personal question, James thought it was just conversation. "I've done well for myself, Mr. Bohan. I own a seafood wholesale business, which I intend to sell."

"Profitable?"

"Very. One of my best employees offered to buy it. He has a wealthy uncle who'll help him."

"How much do you think you'll get out of it?"

"On a fifteen-year note, I figure about twelve thousand a month. I also have investments that would bring up…I'd say near twenty a month."

"You're rich."

"A thousandaire, it is, but not rich." James finished his pint.

* * *

Delany, Bernadette, and Moira hovered around the dining room when Jack and James came in. "Mr. Flaherty," Moira said. "How did you get around?"

"Fine. But not enough to keep up with your father."

Jack said, "But he could keep up with you." He indicated Bernadette.

"That sounds like a challenge," she answered.

"Not from me," James said. "I heard about you."

You're both tired," Delany said. "Why don't you clean up, then get something to eat?"

Ollie Savage was at the bar. "Ollie," James said. "Glad you could make it."

"Wouldn't miss it. Get around with Mr. Bohan well?"

"Very well, thank you. May I join you?"

"Another time, maybe. I came to visit Bernadette."

James whispered, "I don't blame you," and went upstairs.

A short while later, he came back downstairs carrying a manila folder and sat at the table.

"Mr. Flaherty," Bernadette said. "I can smell the fresh air on you. We have roast beef with au jus tonight."

"After all the golf, that sounds good."

"So you think you can beat me?"

"Your dad said that, not me."

Her hazel eyes sparkled. "Mr. Flaherty. Would you mind chatting with me after you eat?"

"Of course." After he enjoyed the roast beef plate, James stepped into the parlor to find her seated near the peat fire.

"Sit down." She offered. "May I get you something?"

"I'm fine." He leaned back on the couch.

"Do you mind if I get a whiskey?"

"I've only seen you drink liquor at the disco. But I'll join you with a single malt."

She went around the corner and returned with two whiskeys. "Thanks," he said. "Now what is it you want to say?"

Bernadette moved closer to him and put her hand on his wrist. "James," she whispered. "I'll always remember you. You're kind, a gentleman, you get along with my family, and, no doubt—my God—a very brave man."

"You surprise me," James whispered back. "I'm glad I met you."

She sipped her whiskey. "In the fall, you'll be home in South Carolina, and I'll be in Dingle, but believe me, I'll always remember you."

James extended the manila folder. "Here. Take this. This is my first tablet. Edit and fix it. Make it better. Your father told me you teach English to Gaelic-speaking kids. You must have your shi—er—stuff together.

"Trust," Bernadette answered. "An honor."

Ollie poked his head around the door. "How, you two."

Standing on the dirt road, we were geared up for our next mission.

"Mary," I said to Ardal, "is much better than the other AO's. Not so muddy, no rice farms near the river."

"You make it sound like paradise."

"Compared to Liza, it's a cake walk."

The choppers rolled in. Three lifts. We were on the third. Diesel exhaust smelled stronger than usual; prop wash dustier. The first lift boarded and whisked away. "Don't lock and load until we come in to the LZ," McKenzie said.

"Hey, Ardal," Rickie-Bear said. "You look like us now."

Shea's fatigues had rotted to a thin veneer; his boots showed a muddy tan. He'd hardened with a deep tan and sinewy muscles. His eyes saw far away, a deep stare. Young body with old eyes. Ardal inspected himself, "I didn't realize; so gradual."

"A Delta warrior," Lorenzo said.

"A Celtic warrior," I added.

In the third lift pickup, we flew at a normal altitude—two thousand feet above the mirror-like paddies. We went in to a soft landing, easily on hard ground, allowing us to step out instead of jumping. The rest of the company had formed a perimeter. We joined them before stretching in line. The pace was steady.

"Don't let your guard down," Sam warned. "Stay on the ready."

In less than an hour, we found ourselves five hundred meters from a fairly big river. Captain Turner ordered a halt then sent RIF's (recons in force) toward the water. Lee, McKenzie, and Lorenzo saw two young women rowing a sampan near the forward bank.

"*Lai dei!*" (come here!)

The girls kept rowing without paying attention to the GI's.

"I said, Lai dei, motherfucker!"

They still rowed along the bank. McKenzie fired a warning shot and waved his hand under to emphasize "lai dei."

The young women disobeyed and kept rowing.

McKenzie fired two warning shots and screamed, "Hey! Come here, dammit!"

The girls still kept rowing. Suddenly, Lorenzo fired directly. Lee opened up with his M60. They aimed at the first girl who fell backward from the force of the bullets. The other girl screamed and cried as McKenzie waded out and pulled the sampan to ground. The girl was riddled with bullet holes, and blood sloshed along the sampan's floor.

"Shut up!"

The other girl kept wailing.

"I said shut up, bitch!"

When she continued wailing, Lee drew his .45 pistol and fired two shots, killing the screamer.

In the pool of blood, McKenzie found a straw bag. "Look. Tax receipts. These two were VC tax collectors. "Look here. A pistol." He retrieved it out of a thick plastic bag filled with oil.

"What kind of gun is it?" Lee inquired.

"A P38. And here's a swastika on the back of the barrel."

"That could be a collector's item," Lee said. "I'll be rich."

"What do you mean, I? We."

"Whoa!" Lorenzo said.

Mortars erupted from nowhere. Machine guns followed. "Take cover!"

"Where?"

Pounding on the turf, the explosions had a greater circumference for the fragmentation effect. We scattered the best we could, but we couldn't return fire into the village. The cry for a PZ came from Company CP. Loud! While the mortars had effect, they were off target, and the rifle fired too high. Waiting for pickup seemed like hours, but thirty minutes later the birds came in. We scrambled into the ships with more of us trying to stuff it. Crew chiefs tried to wave us off, but the pilots decided to take the overloaded ships to the sky. We sluggishly climbed up into thinner air, which would buoy us better. Nearing our village, the choppers had to circle at higher altitude. The pilots performed a controlled autorotation for a soft landing.

Later, at Platoon CP we gathered for our personal after-action palaver. I asked, "Do you think killing those girls was necessary?"

"They were enemies in Indian country," Lee said.

"But they weren't armed," I returned. "I know they were tax collectors, and one of them had a pistol, but I don't think it was meant for offense."

Ardal said, "I agree. You could've just pulled the sampan onto the shore like you did after you murdered them!"

"Listen to you guys!" Rickie-Bear piped. "You're gettin' soft on me."

"What are we doing here?" Ardal asked.

"That's easy," Sam interjected. "We're defending Vietnam, The Republic of."

"So our soldiers are getting wasted for Vietnam, The Republic of."

"That's correct. Now let's spread out and clean our gear."

"Doc," said McKenzie. "We need your help."

"Who's we?"

"Lorenzo, Lee, and me."

Joyner asked, "What kind of help?"

"We can't decide who the rightful owner of this here pistol is."

"So?"

"We'd like you to hold it for us."

Doc wiped sweat from his straw-colored hair. "What the fuck, over? Do you realize what you're asking? I carry this bag to save people's lives. Now you're asking me to carry a weapon of war. "No way!"

"But Doc," said Lee. "You're the only one we can trust. If we give it to someone else, or to Brigade, some major or colonel in the rear will steal it."

"I don't like this."

"Please, Thomas," said McKenzie. "It won't be for long."

"I still don't like it. Is it loaded?"

"A full magazine," Lee answered, "Just like the girl had it."

"That makes it even worse. A weapon from an atrocity. I'm a Quaker; you guys know that?"

"This is war," Lorenzo calmly said.

"Look at you guys. Killers. Nineteen-year-old kids killing women."

"If you do this for us, we can give you something you might need or want."

"Peaches. I'll take some peaches."

"Can do. You won't regret it."

"I already do."

* * *

The nipa palms crinkled in the Delta wind, and lemon trees swayed while coconut palms stood tall. Ardal and I had a night off from guard. We sauntered down the village road until we reached the plaster of pairs gate. I pulled out a joint from my shirt pocket.

Ardal nodded. "Is that?"

"Con sa. Yes. I got it from McKenzie. He smokes a lot."

I lit the "J" and passed it to Ardal for the first hit. "Hold it in for a while before blowing out. He obeyed and passed it back. We smoked it down to a short.

I flicked the roach away, saying, "Over here there's so much of this shit."

Ardal's eyes already looked like ice ponds. We slowly headed back to the platoon. "Seems like we'll never get back," Ardal said.

I chuckled. We saw a young woman along the way. She was sweeping her clay yard and glanced at us. Most Vietnamese carefully averted their eyes when confronted by strangers. I said, "*Em minoi co?*" (How are you?)

"*Kham byet.*" (I don't understand.)

"*Ban nuieu toi?*" (How old are you?)

Surprisingly she answered, "*Mui tam.*"

"Eighteen," I said to Shea. "That means seventeen; they count the nine months of gestation."

She licked her lips and looked around as if to make sure none of the neighbors were watching during afternoon naptime. She backed into her doorway and double checked. Then she waved us in with the traditional top-handed motion.

"Boom boom," I said.

She motioned for Ardal to sit in a chair. She pointed for me to sit on the table that served as a bed.

She stroked the hair on my forearm. She sighed, motioned me to remove my shirt, and then directed me to take off my pants and underwear. She stroked my legs, pubic hair, and erection, saying with a smile, "Numbah one!" She opened her legs and raised to receive me. Only a few thrusts, and I exploded. She smiled and looked around for Ardal. She pointed at the door and waved. I dressed and saw Ardal waiting near the gate.

I waved for him to join me, "She wants you next."

Minutes later, he came out the door smiling. "That was grand. Wait until I tell the guys."

"No. Let's keep it our secret."

Returning to the platoon, we heard lively conversation and stopped in. Lieutenant Sam asked, "Where did you two go?"

"To the village."

"Probably smokin' pot," Rickie-Bear offered.

"Listen up," Sam said. "New mission tomorrow. Late morning. LST's."

"A riverine," I said. "At least we don't have to get up early."

Sam said, "Get rest. Flaherty, air mattress."

"Yes sir."

Next morning, we awoke to quacking ducks and rattling nipa palms. We gathered for morning repast. C-rations gave us the pleasure of trading, as each draw captured great interest. We all had our preferences and bartered for them. The larger cans held the entrees; the smaller cans contained various desserts and fruits.

Rickie-Bear loved ham and lima beans; Ardal, the Irishman that he was, favored roast beef and potatoes and boned beef; Lee preferred poultry. McKenzie liked anything but ham and limas. We opened our boxes and began our ritual. We pulled out peanut butter first, for it, when mixed with insect repellent, provided an excellent fuel for heating our entrees. I got beef stew and potatoes—an easy trade with Ardal because he drew boned chicken. McKenzie drew the seasoned beef, Lee drew boned chicken, his favorite, and Rickie-Bear found boned turkey.

We used the P-38's from our dog tags to open the entrees just halfway so we could hold the cans over the peanut butter heat. Everyone was satisfied until we opened our fruits and cakes: "What the fuck, over! No peaches in any of 'em!"

About an hour before the mission, Sam approached with a new guy. "Men, I want you to meet Bernard Bernstein. He's not going to join us this morning, but we'll get more acquainted later."

The brown-water boats appeared. The front gates were lowered for us to board. Ardal and I stood together as the boats slowly traveled about forty-five minutes to our destination.

Gun boats provided security.

"Look at those things," Ardal said, "They're loaded up."

"I'll say. 60s, 50s, automatic grenade launchers, and those flame throwers—crispy critters!"

We landed on the bank and splashed out. Each squad had an air mattress carrier to cross the endless canals. I was designated carrier for ours. When we reached the first canal, we blew up the air mattresses to float our weapons and gear across, pushed and guided by two of us, one on each side. Then deflated and moved on, a tedious routine. We sank in the rice paddy mud too often, slowing our progress and tiring us even more. Ardal sank up to his waist again. I helped him out with the barrel of my rifle set on safety. When we reached a berm and rested, Ardal said, "While we're out here in this shit, what do you think the REMF's (Rear Echelon Mother Fuckers) are doing right now?"

I answered, "Probably eating steaks and drinking beer."

"It just ain't fair."

"Nothins' fair. But if I were them, I'd be doin' the same thing."

We continued slogging through the mud; resting on every berm until we reached our destination close to a big river. We settled on a line and stretched along the bank; time for a long rest; time for talk. The sky began burning orange toward the end of the day.

"That was a tough one," Lee said, sweat pouring from his closely cropped brown hair. "Is that gun safe with you, Doc?"

"Could you hurry up and decide who owns it? I'm going to turn it over to CP after this."

"Don't do that. We'll figure it out."

We broke open our C's to eat them cold in the 'bush.' Ardal drew ham and limas,

"Ugh!" I drew boned turkey. We both tossed them back into the box and pulled out the fruit and cake. I got fruit cocktail and marble pound cake; Shea put his applesauce back.

"Hey Ardal." I said. "You know marble cake and fruit cocktail go together."

"Lucky you."

"Don't get down, brother. I'll share. Open one of those big cans and throw out whatever it is, and we can mix the fruit and cake together: some for me, some for you."

"Thanks bro"

We settled into the dusk. Word came for a two-hour watch; Ardal and I would guard together. The same unsettled feeling came over us, and from our eyes, the thousand yard stare. Ardal whispered softly, "We've come all this way and nothing happened. Do you think we're safe?"

"Remember the farmers we saw? Rest assured, they'll be soldiers at night. So watch."

We relaxed briefly. Every once in a while, we'd hear a large lizard swishing by or the rushing tide. Dawn came quietly as across the line, soldiers stirred. Snowy egrets gathered in their usual clusters on bony trees. Shea and I rubbed our eyes and yawned. I had been assigned to watch out for him, train him, show him the ropes every new guy needed, and I was satisfied with my work. He was no longer a new guy. His clothes rotted like ours, and he'd turned tan and muscular like the savages we'd become; forty-year-old-eyes in a twenty-year-old man. He was one of us now. A brother.

The far left flank was suddenly rocked by an explosion. We could hear moans and screams.

A soldier from the second platoon came running to company. "A VC set off a claymore; two dead, four wounded!"

We heard M16's wildly firing. Concussion grenades thrown into the river. Explosions mumphed! Men crying and screaming. Medics rushed to the wounded.

Turner cried through the radio. "Dust-off! Dust-off!"

We could only sit helplessly while this drama unfolded. The rifle-fire ceased, and we heard a yell. "Charlie got away; that zipperhead bastard." The medivac came and carried away casualties while we fired into empty space. The rain began; misty at first, then steady, as we collected ourselves and settled. We could now hear quiet sobbing.

I said to Ardal, "I wonder who it was. No, I don't want to know."

After two hours, we continued our mission. As the rain came harder, we moved southwest to more canals and knee-deep mud. The tide was now rushing out, and we crossed two more canals, each with swift currents. We finally reached a wider canal. Air mattresses inflated again, and we started to cross. Ardal motioned for Joyner and me to cross first along with Lee and Rickie-Bear. On our side we waited for Ardal and McKenzie to bring the air mattress and gear across. In the rushing water, the air mattress started to deflate. Ardal and McKenzie clung as tightly as they could, but the sides were too soft, and water splashed across, choking them. The current pulled at them as they clung harder, but grips slipping, the mattress started downstream, completely deflated. Joyner waded in from shore and tried to arrest the floating vessel. The two soldiers, choking and coughing, were carried in the current, and their struggles to stay above water began to fail. Further downstream, they grasped for nipa roots. Doc waded faster, the mattress completely gone, and tried to rescue them. He saw two farmers approach. Desperate now, he tried to hold the bag above water. The farmers saw him and the drowning GI's. Two carbines pointed. Joyner yelled, trying to scare them away. The enemy moved closer to the shore and raised their rifles. Doc pulled the pistol from his medical bag and remembered Lee telling him it was locked and loaded. He fumbled with the safety, then pointed and fired—fired—fired! He heard machine guns. Rickie-Bear and Lee came running to the shore. Together they yanked and hauled McKenzie and Ardal from the water, Doc shoving from below. McKenzie shook his head and gasped. Ardal lay still.

I ran to him and lifted his head. "NO, NO. Not like this!"

"Mouth to mouth," said Doc. "I'll pump."

We worked hard on him. We knew he'd be brain damaged or worse without air.

"C'mon, Ardal," I said. "Stay with us. Stay with us."

While Joyner pumped, I pulled Ardal's elbows. "Listen to me. Dammit, I'm not going to let you go!"

Shea suddenly gurgled water. He turned his head and coughed. I kissed him on the chin, forehead, and each cheek. "I love you, brother. I love you."

Joyner carried each soldier's rifles. He raised them high. He raised the P38 and kissed it, then he raised one of the M16's and declared, "I'm going to get one of these from the armorer."

It was an October afternoon. James rubbed his strained eyes, leaned back in the chair, and took a deep breath and yawned. *This is getting too hard. Maybe I should go home and finish. I can type it up and send it to the Shea's. I lost my editor and feel like I'm wearing out my welcome.*

Bernadette had been gone two months now. He still longed for her and wondered if she felt the same. He would never know. He would quietly leave. He hadn't prepared for winter weather; he came during May, never expecting to be here so long. It was definitely time to go. He began to pack. He would drive to Dublin and turn in the rental.

Catching a flight there needed no advance reservation. He went downstairs to speak to Delany about leaving. She smiled when she saw him.

He greeted her. "You're happy this evening. Good news?"

"Meat market low, meat market flows."

"Can we talk about me settling up?"

Her smile checked, but she winked and pointed to the dining room.

He crossed into the dining room and was shocked to see Bernadette sitting at a table. She looked up and smiled. She was radiant. He beamed. "You're sure a fine thing today! May I sit?"

"Certainly."

She stretched her hand to his and gripped.

"So this is why your mother is smiling! Her daughter came home; for how long?"

"This is the October bank holiday at the end of autumn."

"Never heard of it. How long?"

"Three days.

"How are you going to spend them?"

"I invited my dear friends over for some craic."

"Will you spare me some time?" Rethinking his plan to leave.

"Depends on what you have to offer."

"Yuh. Go ahead. Be with your dear friends. I'll go back to work."

"And pack for your flight home?"

"Oh?"

"James. You've been here six months. Your visa expired. You have to go."

She smiled so warmly. "Come, sit with me a while?"

They settled in the den.

"Let's have a shot for all the good times."

"I'll join you, sir. The peat fire cast a warm glow onto Bernadette's hair and face. God, girl. You're so beautiful. I'm going to miss you."

She raised her glass. "I will you, as well."

James toasted and said, "Before we start, I…think…I would… forget it."

Bernadette's eyes moistened. "And?"

He saw her pulse quicken; his heart was pounding. He was confused and caught between joy and terror, never having felt so hopeful and at the same time powerless. He forced out, "Have fun with the girls. Tell them hello for me," and rose.

"Please reconsider! They'd love having you."

He turned with a wooden smile. *What am I doing?* and climbed back up the stairs to his room.

* * *

Her friends arrived together out of the autumn chill and settled in the den. They bubbled, laughed, talked about latest news, and told jokes until James appeared, holding his suitcase in the doorway.

"James!" Harper blurted. "You're leaving us."

"Time to go," he said matter of factly.

"Oh," said Ellsbeth. "Please stay a while."

"We're going to miss you," Caroline said.

"I've enjoyed y'all. You've made my visit wonderful. I do appreciate it."

Bernadette then said, "Why don't you wait for tomorrow? You'll have to drive those narrow roads in the night."

"That's right. We wouldn't want anything happen to you." It was Harper again. "Stay here and gargle with us!" She raised her glass.

They giggled. "We're going to miss you."

He stood thinking, then settled his suitcase on the floor. "Okay. You convinced me."

"Yay! Sit," Bernadette said. "I'll get you another whiskey."

"Thanks." He sat quietly, enjoying the gossiping and chuckling and outbursts of laughter. He admired them. Each of them glanced at him; Bernadette smiled and began to stare. "Bernadette," he said. "Why don't we dance for the last time?"

"We don't have any music."

"We can hum along. How about it?"

So they both stood up, girlfriends clapping, and closed in the dance. He hummed "Magic Moment." "This magic moment. So distant and so new. I know you felt it, by the look in your eyes."

She joined in the words, "Sweeter than wine. Softer than the summer nights."

He sang, "And then it happened, when your lips were close to mine." He lifted her chin and looked into her eyes. "I can have everything, everything 'til the end of time."

She teared up and sung softly, "Till the end of time."

He dropped to one knee. "Bernadette Caitlin Bohan, would you do me the honor of becoming my wife?"

Silence. Shock. Sobered. The girls traded glances, and then there was more clapping and hugging.

Bernadette held back tears and said, "Yes! Oh yes."

Harper cried out, "G'wan, G'wan!"

Clapping and cheering. The couple drew close together and passionately kissed. James grasped the top of her hand, placed his over, and held them above their shoulders.

"Oh Bernadette. We're going to miss you when you move to the States."

"We're not going to," James replied. "We're goin' to settle in Ireland! I'm going to apply for citizenship."

* * *

"Utopian mirage.

"Huh?"

"It's like a utopian mirage, you and me.

"James. I didn't know you were so romantic."

"I didn't either, so early in the morning."

She peered around the cabin of the aircraft. "I've never flown before."

"Nervous?"

"A little. But I feel this is an adventure."

"Six hours to Boston."

She shifted in her seat and looked across the aisle at other passengers.

James said, "I remember my first couple of flights; white knuckle on takeoff and landing." He knew she would be anxious, like the feeling of being in a tube; hearing the loud whine of jet engines; the casual movement of others in their seats. As the aircraft slowly backed out of the gate, he noticed beads of sweat across her forehead. Turning onto the runway, the plane blew out its engines and thrust a roar for takeoff.

She gripped her seat handles as the aircraft slowly rose into the sky. The color came back to her face. She gazed out the window and felt the lift as the plane made a wide turn above the morning clouds.

James said, "Would you like a blanket?"

"That would be lovely. Quite an experience."

"So," he returned, "Comfortable now? We have about six hours to Boston. Cover yourself and relax."

"Yes, and James." She smiled, "Keep your hands on top of it."

"Yes, me ashmi."

She leaned her head on his shoulder and began to relax. He reached under the blanket and squeezed her black stocking thigh. "Ahh, feels good."

He said, "Do you realize we've only known each other a little more than six months?"

She rubbed his arm. "What attracted you to me?"

"Intelligence. I love intelligent women. You're well-educated. Good with language, and have a witty sense of humor."

"Do I look good?"

"Absolutely."

"Am I beautiful?"

"Gorgeous. What attracted you to me?"

Without a pause, he said, "Much the same. Your looks at first. I love your wavy brown hair and your face. But most of all your eyes—deep blue and penetrating. I felt you saw through me, like undressing me."

The stewardess came by. "Would you like anything to drink?"

"Do you have Coke?" Bernadette answered.

The stewardess looked at them and smiled.

They dozed off, and, in what seemed like a short time, the flight approached Logan Airport in Boston. The plane banked into a smooth landing. As the passengers disembarked, James told Bernadette, "We should probably get you some clothes for the milder weather in Carolina. We have enough time here."

She tried different outfits. Of course, she looked good in every style she picked.

When they landed in Charlotte, James' neighbor gathered them up in his pickup truck. "Hey, Tom. Thanks for getting us. This is my fiancée, Bernadette Bohan. Bernadette, this is my neighbor, Tom O'Leary."

"A fine Irish name, it is."

Tom said, "Fiancée? How in the world did you snare Jimmy? We thought he'd never get married." He turned the radio to a classic rock station called THE RIDE.

Between sets, the disc jockey exclaimed, "The songs of your life! THE RIDE!"

Bernadette covered her mouth and tried to hold back a chuckle.

"Am I missin' somethin' here?" Tom asked.

"I'll tell ya later," James said.

She watched the countryside as farms and lakes passed by. The sun had a wavering effect. She said, "I forgot you drive on the wrong side of the road."

The men laughed.

"That's right," Tom said. "We do it right over here."

A little less than an hour, they arrived at James' house in Columbia.

"My, what a big one!"

The men laughed again. "That's right, partner. Welcome to America."

Tom helped them unload, then he said, "Don't forget the cookout tomorrow evening. Food and dancing."

"It's still warm for November."

"The forecast calls for mid-seventies next week."

"Two sets of golf clubs." Tom noticed the second golf bag. "She plays?"

"She's good."

* * *

Jimmy, as his friends called him, immediately opened the windows and turned on the ceiling fans.

"Early morning, whew. Let's lie down and rest. Pick a room."

She chose one of the extra rooms, settled her bags on the floor, and herself on the bed. After reliving parts of the exciting day, she fell asleep in the warm evening, hearing crickets outside.

She stretched, yawned. The next morning, she heard James padding down the hall to the kitchen. Shortly after, he knocked on the door. "Coffee ready."

Standing in the kitchen, she sipped the welcome cup. "Today is Saturday. I can't see to any business 'til Monday. Let's get going, and do some things."

They went to the old Pancake House for breakfast. Waiting in line, he told her, "I forgot the other thing that attracted me about you—your hazel eyes turning different shades. I'm trying to put together your mood for each color."

"Did you come up with anything? I have no idea."

"It seems your light brown represents stability, blue for contentment, and green for passion."

"Flaherty? Two. Follow me," and they were shown to a small table.

Looking over the menu, she said, "What a variety. I don't know what all this is. I see omelets, potatoes, and grits?"

"Most popular in the South. But this is a pancake house. Why don't you try potato cakes?"

"They have boxties?"

"That's what I'm going to get."

"Me too."

"After we eat," Jimmy said, "We can go to my old school. It's a beautiful campus."

"You are, too," she returned. "This is the first time I've seen you in shorts. You have nice legs. Are we going to send messages, too?"

"Yes. A couple of things we'll need for the beach."

He took her to the University of South Carolina. In the warm noonday sun, they walked along the Horseshoe, where old brick and stone masonry graced the walkways, benches, and trees. "It is beautiful."

"Yep, maybe like Trinity, but much younger. C'mon, let's go send messages."

He drove to a Piggly Wiggly.

"Is that a store?"

"Grocery. We'll get some beer for tonight and a few things for the beach on Monday."

"That's a cute name for a grocery store."

"I have an idea," Jimmy said. "They have t-shirts and sweatshirts. Maybe we can get them for Harper, Ellsbeth, and Caroline. They'll get a kick out of them."

"Ellsbeth especially. She likes things like that."

They also went to a clothing store where she bought white capris and two blouses. She asked, "Do these look good for a cookout and the green tie-dye?"

"Maybe blue jeans and long sleeves. It could turn cool after dark."

They returned to the house for the rest of the afternoon. The sheer curtains gently fluttered in the cool breeze as she noticed through the bay windows in the living room the trees were losing their leaves. Only the fall hedges and plants gave off color.

"You lived all your life with this," Bernadette said.

"Not really. I grew up in Pennsylvania; I moved here when I was seventeen. It's been my home since then.

"Ireland will be your new home. Let's rest away the afternoon." They went upstairs to the king bed and lay side by side. She smoothed his hair. "Jimmy, do you remember when I returned from Dingle that day?"

"How can I ever forget?"

"I want to tell you something, something very important. I had a fella over there for more than two years. His name is Devlin Power. He's a good man. You put me into a conundrum; I had to make a choice. I know Devlin had plans for us: marriage, family, and a life together. We both taught at the intermediate school. I did it to him. I was so embarrassed and sad for it. I didn't want to hurt him, but I did. He almost cried. I didn't tell him about you. It was so hard."

"You knew I was goin' to propose?"

"I was hoping."

Jimmy replied, "You did that for me? Even though you hardly knew me?"

"I fell hard for you, Jimmy. I had to do it, and I just hoped you would accept me. When you proposed, it was my happiest moment," her eyes welling up.

Jimmy embraced her. "I'm happy, too. I love you."

* * *

The O'Leary's house perched above a lake. They had three decks: a screened porch over the lake, a small deck leaning beside the garage, and the larger one from glass sliding doors, where it was adorned with several torch lights and candles to keep the bugs away. When Jimmy and Bernadette arrived, they were instantly greeted.

"Welcome," said Sadie O'Leary, extending her arms for a hug. "So this is your fiancée, Jimmy. Let me take a look at you, honey. Whoa. Wawkin' the Dawg!" She added, "You must be somethin' special to snare Jimmy boy; we thought he would never get married."

Bernadette nodded. "We brought you this beer to share."

"I 'clare. He thinks of everything. Go on; get ya some eats."

Bernadette explored the buffet. She saw sliced tomatoes with mozzarella and fresh basil, baked beans, pulled pork, fried chicken, hamburgers, and hotdogs. "Looks great," she said to Jimmy. "I'll have it all."

"Not too much pork. I'm taking you to a barbecue house tomorrow."

Other guests came trickling in, all anxious to meet Jimmy's new fiancée. While eating, Bernadette engaged in lively conversation. He saw her nodding and smiling. Tom approached James and asked, "So tell me, Jimmy. When I picked y'all up in Charlotte, why was she giggling about The Ride?"

"In Irish slang, ride means fucking."

"Oh? And are you?"

"Too personal, Tommy, too personal. We just became engaged."

"Where are you two fixin' to live?"

"Ireland, for sure."

"We'll sure miss you around here."

* * *

Jimmy, in animated conversation with a group, at one point, blurted, "What the fuck, over!"

Bernadette said, "James! Your language!"

"I'm just being myself."

"You're not there anymore."

Jimmy kissed her cheek. "Thank you."

"Okay, y'all! Time to boogie! Let's dance!" Sadie turned on a prepared tape. "Yay!" "Dance to the Music" by Sly came on. "C'mon, girl, show me how you dance!" She pulled Bernadette to the center of the deck and started to wave and kick. Bernadette followed along, swinging her hips and her arms in the air. A few more dancers followed. "Proud Mary" blasted the speakers, and then just about everybody was throwin' down. So many familiar songs, so many dancers, so much laughter. The party roared on, and when Aretha Franklin played, Bernadette noticed a couple dancing.

"Jimmy," she whispered, "What do you call that?"

"The leg. Hey, Charles! Why don't you show Bernadette how to do the leg; I'll take Marinda."

Bernadette got the hang of it very quickly. She lunged forward and drew back, as if she'd known the moves all her life. "Higher" brought the dancers closer to the middle of the deck, their hands raised, reaching into the dark sky. Then "Takin' Care of Business" and "I'll Survive." As the tape kept rolling, they then leaned into beach music and the Shag. James and his fiancée danced easily. Her eyes revealed delight as they moved together. A slow set started, which brought all the couples onto the dance floor. The torch lights cast a soft light over them, and "This Magic Moment" widened Bernadette's eyes. She closed to a tight hug with James, cheek to cheek, whispering, and finally kissing. The dancers rested after that.

"This is grand," she told James.

"I'm having a ball. Another beer?"

"Two is enough for me."

A guy came staggering in out of the dark. He tripped over the top step of the deck and raised his voice, "Great party!"

"Arnold, where's Lizzy?" Tom asked him.

He pointed. "Out yonder on the grass."

"Is she drunk?"

"Havin' a large time."

Tom said, "Why don't you sit down? Here."

Sadie went out to the lawn to collect Lizzie. The dancers chuckled and watched Arnold stumble to a soft chair and slump in. "Whoa, Arnold. Havin' a large time?" As it was getting late, guests began to head for home.

Bernadette asked Jimmy, "Did they break the party?"

"About to end, anyway. Why don't we go back to the house?"

* * *

Lying on top of the bedspread, Bernadette sighed. "I'm sure glad I only had a beer and a half. I wouldn't want to get ossified like your friend."

"Just an acquaintance."

"He talked different from the rest."

"He and Lizzie are from Calhoun County. That's the way they talk down there."

"We certainly left a mess over there."

"Let's go over tomorrow and help clean up."

"Perfect. I'd like to thank them for the mighty craic. Especially the music. I loved the music. When we girls took off our shoes to "Dancing in the Moonlight"—a real gas. And our song, thank you."

"I reckon I should be thankin' you."

She paused, "James, can we talk a bit?"

"Anytime. What's on your mind, girl?"

"I heard you talking to Tom about living in Ireland, but this is your home, isn't it?"

"Not anymore. I have a new home, and I can't wait to return."

She kissed him. "You don't know how much that means to me." Her hair spread out on the pillow. "Do you think we could go to your hometown before we go home?"

"Why?"

"I think it's important to see where you grew up. How far is it?"

"About seven hundred miles. It would take some planning." He added, "I'd have to change the flight. O'Leary's keeping the car for sale, so we'd have to rent one. It'll be a long drive."

"How long?"

"About ten hours."

"That long!?"

"We're a big country. Hell, it would take us six days to get to California. I know, I've done it twice."

Her fingers were on the back of his neck, ruffling his hair. "I read in your memoir that you and Ardal rode Vietnamese girls."

"And?"

"Were they good rides?"

"Bernadette Caitlin Flaherty. You'll be the best and only ride of my life. I'm yours forever."

She leaned and kissed him on the cheek.

"Come here, girl." He surrounded her with his arms and gave her a deep kiss.

She responded with her tongue but pulled back. "James, I want to wait. I'm sorry, love, but I'm just not ready for this." She slipped off his bed and returned to her room.

James woke up first Sunday morning, and knocked softly on her door. "Hey, sleepy, let's get ready to help Tom and Sadie clean up."

* * *

They were busy sweeping the deck when she and James arrived. They pitched in until the job was done.

"Thanks for the wonderful time," she said to Sadie. "I loved the food and dancing."

"We loved having you," Sadie replied. "And I'm so glad I met you. I like your charm and hope you and Jimmy will have a wonderful life together."

"You two have plans today?" Tom asked.

"Southern barbecue."

"Sounds great. When will we see you again?"

"Tomorrow, for sure. I'm going to sign the business note at the attorney's office and set up the sale of all my property. I trust you'll still handle my car and house for me."

"My pleasure," said Tom. "How are you gonna handle the money?"

"I'm going to open an account at the Bank of Ireland when I get home."

"Home," Sadie said. "It sounds exciting to me that you're going to live in Ireland."

"We're going to love it," Jimmy replied. "I'm very excited."

"Until then. Enjoy your time in South Carolina, Bernadette."

"I already am."

Walking back to the car, she said, "Jimmy, I don't want to go to the barbecue. Could we do something else?"

"No barbecue? Well, how 'bout a round? The course I like to play doesn't get busy until after church. That gives us up to 10:30 a.m. or so before it gets crowded."

* * *

They stood on the first tee at Linrick Golf Course. "I can play the senior tee. It's always close to the women's tee."

She said, "I can play men's tee."

"Sure? Some of the holes are long."

"I can play deadly."

"This is a par-five, down a slope, slightly dog-leg left.

Bernadette reached into her bag. "I'll use the three. I hit it better. What will we play for?"

"A bet?"

"That's what golf is meant for. So, how 'bout it?"

"Choice for dinner tonight?"

"You're on." She lined up her three-wood and hit with fine form. The ball went straight with a slight draw, rolling an extra thirty yards.

"I think we'll be eating dinner at your choice."

James struck his driver to the right of the fairway. They silently walked to their second shots. "I usually hit a mid iron," James said. "That'll get me inside the one-fifty marker."

"I think I'll hit a wood, if you don't mind." She landed about fifty yards from the green, longer than his one-thirty yard shot. Both hit the green and made pars. Bernadette barely missed the birdie putt.

Number two par-three played 145 downhill. "You don't need a one-fifty club. The pin's red. In the front."

She hit the eight-iron club. He used a nine-iron club. He found himself in the left hand bunker, while she went pin-high right.

"See those pine trees over that cart path? Sometimes crows hang out, waiting for golfers to leave their carts. They drop down and steal any food they might find. Newer golfers don't know that."

"Magpies do that, too. They're smart birds."

"Yuh. They're cunning thieves."

James' sandblast left him in the right rough past the green. Bernadette again almost made her birdie. He bogeyed.

"One up," she said.

"First blood," he answered. "I don't like this next hole."

"Not good enough for it?"

"No. It's just the way it's set up."

They both hit their threes, landing on the flat at one-fifty.

"See what I mean? Downhill lies over a pond. This hole gives me fits."

"Be brave. Surely your war experience made you brave."

"Not on the golf course." He hit eight-iron just across the pond, but short of the green.

She hit six onto the green under the hole.

"Damn, Bernadette; that was perfect. What kind of food do you like best?"

"Italian."

James had to chip onto the green, a bit too long for a comfortable putt. She made her uphill for a birdie. She jumped up and down and squealed. James three putted for a double.

Jack was right, James thought. *She's not only good, but great at the game.*

Seven-irons to the back pin on par-three number four; both left with long uphill putts. James started thinking about Italian restaurants in town. They both parred.

"Two up now," she said with a wink. "Let's move on, lad."

"This is the longest hole on the course," James explained. "Try to hit to the left so you don't roll to the right. Danger there."

She used a driver over the middle with a fade.

He said, "Uh-oh."

"What do ye mean, uh-oh?"

"You're gonna be on the rocks."

They walked over the first hill. To the right, James clung to the fairway, and Bernadette was on the rocks.

She saw it and said, "I like my whiskey straight."

"You can take it off the rocks and find a place to drop it."

"That violates the rules."

"Are we playing for big money? We have two rules here: drop from the rocks; drop from the roots."

She launched a five-wood over the trees. He hit four wood farther left. When they reached their balls, she said, "Deep forest around here. Do ye get a drop outta there?"

"Of course not. See that wood line over on the right? An old guy went hawking balls and got bit by a copperhead snake. They had to bring a helicopter in."

"Like a dust off in the Mekong Delta? Did he succumb?"

"He sued."

"Why?"

"Old guys. Probably depression child out to get whatever he can."

"I'm glad we don't have snakes in Ireland."

"I won't ever have to see them again," James answered. "Let's move on before one of those no-shoulders comes after us."

She had to pitch to a blue flag. *Ok. See how she handles this.* She pitched it within a foot of the pin. *Damn! She can do anything. What a golfer!*

They rounded to ten.

"Where's this hole?" Bernadette asked.

"It's blind over the hill. Try to hit down the middle."

She lofted a high three-wood as he instructed. He hit his to the left.

"Now, you're on the rocks," she gloated. "Ye need a whiskey, do ye?"

"I can deal with it." He managed to roll it on the green.

"Nice shot, James. I didn't think you could do it."

On the next tee, James went into his bag, pulled out a pack of crackers, and began to crush them. "Whatta ya doin' now, carlow?"

"I'm going to call Charlie. Char-char-char-char!"

"I don't see anyone. Huh?"

"Here he comes."

"A feckin' duck?"

"Charlie." He spread the crumbs around, and Charlie waddled in and swooped them up.

"Ugly duck."

"A Muscovy. Very ugly, but, like you, a great breast."

"You feckin' gobshite!"

Bernadette again hit a high, arching three wood past the one-fifty. James' fell shorter. They reached the green, where she made birdie and he par. They worked their way to the thirteenth fairway. "See that shed over there?" He pointed. "That used to be a stable for horses."

"Run down, is it."

"Sometimes a guy with his girlfriend would stop play, wave people through, and go to the barn to fuck."

"That's deadly. You're not—-"

"I'm always thinking."

On fourteen tee, James said, "Par five. Could be birdie or even an eagle. Or a feckin' disaster. Try hittin' a hook around those trees up there. You could run down the bottom and have short iron to the green. To the right, you're dead in the woods."

Bernadette hit four-wood around the trees.

First time on the course and she hit the perfect shot. Wow!

James reached the top for a flat lie. All he had to do was punch an iron and join her ball. Walking up the hill, she said, "All these hills are wearing me out."

"The worst is yet to come. Maybe we should slow down the pace."

She glanced to the woods. "Maybe go back to that shed?"

Once they reached the top, she touched his arm. "Jimmy. I read when you saved Ardal from drowning. Did you intend religious allegory?"

"I barely know what an allegory is, only mentioned in high school."

"I think it is. Maybe you didn't know it, but it's still there."

"I just wrote about what actually happened."

"O mo dia!" She saw her ball perched on a tuft of grass at the bottom of the hill. "You were right. There it is."

"Mine's right with ye. I lie two. You lie one."

She hit a wedge on the green. He did also.

"You have a fifteen footer. It'll break slightly left. You make it, you got yourself an eagle." She came up two inches short. Another birdie. James three-putted for a bogey. He said, "You're killing me."

At fifteen tee, he pointed out where the riding trails were, even across the fairway. "Don't hit yet!"

"Why?'

"Those deer there. They'll be crossing the fairway."

She watched. "There's three, no five of 'em. Beautiful."

"They'll cross over the crick and up the hill. Sometimes you can see where they sleep on the next hole. We have a flock of wild turkeys that show up from time to time."

She hit the five-wood to the left, dangerously near the crick and woods.

"Uh-oh. You'll have to hook around those trees."

As he teed his ball, she said, "I still think you meant it for allegory."

"I promise you, I didn't know."

"It was perfect."

Sixteen, the monster par-five, had a double dogleg. They reached the plateau easily. She saw the large pond they had to hit over. "What a feckin' disaster. What should I do?"

"Do what you've been doing. Hit a good one, high as you can." After two bogies, they reached the par-three seventeenth. "Where are the goats?" she looked around.

"There're no goats around here. Just the feckin crows."

They continued the round and finished eighteen. She scored eighty-two; he, eighty-six, "Four up. Huh-huh."

"Quit braggin.' Let's load up and go home."

They drove home and cleaned up. Sitting together in the kitchen, James said, "You're wonderful. I'm so happy I met you. You're good at everything."

"I don't know," she answered.

"We'll find out when we marry."

"There's an Italian place downtown called Divino Rosso. I'll take you there tonight."

"Interesting! *Probebilmente solo un bicchiere di vino rosso.*"

"Huh?"

* * *

Six thirty, and well-recovered from the round of golf, they sat at a plush, white-clothed table at Divino's. Secluded with pale rosy light. "I don't remember that necklace," James pointed out.

"It's ruby, my birthstone. Remember when we went to Waterford City? I bought it then. "I had to do the goo."

"What's that?"

"Compare prices."

"It's beautiful."

"I saved it for special occasions. Hey, I liked that twisted par-five on the back. What a hard hole!"

"Hardest on the course. You didn't hit any in the water. I'll tell you something, Bernadette. We're a great couple. All our lives we can enjoy each other's company, and I'm looking forward to it."

The waiter approached. "My name is Gregorio. Would like something to drink?" He had an Italian accent. A student, James surmised.

Bernadette said, "*Si. Barola Anno.*"

Gregorio smiled. Ah! *Vino rosso?*"

"Si. *Y polpette al sugo.*"

"Ahh. Very good.

"*Y Formaggi.*"

"Wow," James said. "You speak Italian."

"A little."

"What did you order?"

"Barola. A red wine. Ok?"

"What was that other stuff?"

"Cured meats and assorted cheese." Her eyes twinkled. Her face glowed in the low light. Her skin had tanned, and her hair seemed to be a deeper auburn.

"You're staring at me."

"Yuh, I am."

The plates came with cured meats, cheeses, and toast points.

"Perfect."

They ate quietly. The wine arrived. The waiter poured a taste for her.

She swirled, sniffed, and took a small swallow. "Brix a bit low, but perfect."

"What in the hell is brix?"

"Sugar to acid balance. The lower the brix, the higher the acid."

The waiter poured for each of them.

She took the first full swallow. "Barola is a small town in the eastern Piedmont of Italy. It's the most prized of all Italian wines."

He swallowed. "Good."

When it came time to order, she said, "*Pappardelle alla bolognese*. You, James?"

He struggled. "Spaghetti and meatballs!"

"Oh, James. Let me order for you! Live a little. Vitello di marsala."

"I hope it's good."

"You'll love it."

* * *

Back at his house, relaxing on the porch chairs, she said, "Exhausted. Should sleep well."

"Sweetie, how do you know so much about food and wine?"

"I dated a man in Dublin who was very cosmopolitan. I learned from him, and I'm familiar with languages."

"Was he a student?"

"A restaurateur. A great learning experience. We went out a year or so."

They talked quietly and watched the light change as the sky darkened.

She caught her head drooping and admitted. "Bedtime for me. Great day and fun tomorrow."

They rose and went to their separate rooms.

* * *

James drove them to Myrtle Beach. He'd signed the promissory note with the purchase at his lawyer's office. The O'Leary's would handle the sale of his house and cars. They were three hours on back roads before arriving in Myrtle Beach, the best place to be for young beachgoers in South Carolina. He had rented a small, wooden house across the street from a busy pavilion.

"Quaint!" Bernadette declared, hands on her hips.

James answered, "One bedroom, one bathroom, and a small living room. Quaint, indeed."

She came out of the bathroom wearing a bikini. "How do I look?"

"I'll need to keep you close to me; every man on the beach will be gawking."

"Isn't that what it's for?"

They made their way across the sand and stood on the wide, flat beach.

"Beautiful. Such smooth sand and so many people."

They found a place to sit. She waded into the water, splashed around, and dove in a couple of times. Her wet skin was shiny in the sun. Her bikini revealed more of her than James would like, and he glanced up and down the beach, relieved that no one seemed to be looking. They hung out until late afternoon, splashing and diving and holding hands while strolling in the wet sand. He said, "I think it's time to go back. We'll come back in the morning, with some chairs and an umbrella."

"That was wonderful," she said. "I never saw a beach so wide."

"I never saw a girl so beautiful."

"You're so sleeven, James."

They rested until dusk then dressed for dinner. She slid on her knee-length split skirt, and he wore shorts and a blue collared shirt. They held hands and walked to a seafood restaurant. After a ten minute wait, they were seated in the middle of the restaurant. "All that salt air made me hungry," she said. "What do you recommend?"

"I'm going—"

"What's this!?"

"Frogmore stew. That's what I'm going to have."

"Does it have frogs in it?"

"No. Read it."

"Shrimp, sausage, corn, and potatoes. What a weird combination. What do you think is the fish of the day? I like ling or haddock."

He smiled. "I don't think you'll find that here. How about fish and chips?"

She slowly perused. "They use flounder for fish and chips. I like flat fish."

"Would you like a glass of wine?"

"White."

James ordered Sauvignon Blanc for them. Then he told the young waitress, "Frogmore stew, please."

Bernadette said, "I'll wait for the wine before I choose." She looked around. The place was adorned with small anchors, large ropes, and round, ship-like windows. "I feel like I'm actually in a ship."

"You look like you're topside. Your tan is developing, and it looks grand."

"Okay. I'll try the frogs. It will be a new experience."

After dinner, they made a short drive to North Myrtle Beach and visited The Pad, where beach dancing, the Shag, dominated. The floor was covered with a light sprinkling of powder to complement the dancing. They joined the large crowd there and danced to beach music, enjoying the atmosphere where the dance started. Bernadette had learned well from Sadie. She and Jimmy connected as they turned and stepped together. When Ben E. King sang with a slow beat, they broke from the Shag, and, like some others on the dance floor, slow-danced to "Stand By Me." "This is a beautiful song," she sighed.

"Do you know who that singer is?" He smiled, "The same man who recorded our song."

They danced steadily without a break. That was the beauty of the place—his arm around her waist, her cheek on his neck. When they danced apart, their eyes were fixed on one another. Coordinated smoothly, they were quite a match. "Let's go home."

James said. "I'm getting tired."

"Me, too."

* * *

In the morning, they dressed for the beach. He took her to the pavilion across the street, where he bought a small beach chair and umbrella. They grabbed a hotdog and a Coke. They set up on the beach. "I'll let you rub the lotion on me, Jimmy. I feel a wee bit invigorated."

He enjoyed feeling her body; he applied the lotion slowly. "Hmmm, so smooth."

Morning clouds capped the shore, and a moon tide ushered in a cool breeze for the sun bathers. The waves sparkled, and the sky seemed to heat the horizon. As James walked along the beach, she watched through her sunglasses how easily he chatted with people. No one was a stranger to him. She remembered a biology professor at Trinity who gave a full lecture on the human connection with the sea. He talked about how the salts had associated each other: the human body needed salt, amniotic fluid was mostly salt, the blood in veins were mostly salt, and the ocean covered more than seventy percent of the earth. He reasoned all life sprang from the ocean, and every animal evolved from it. She could see how plausible it could be. She had a strong connection with James. She liked the way he carried himself. He was a strong man, but with a gentle side that made her feel good about herself—a certain élan for life she loved. He truly was a Celtic warrior, but within, the gentle soul of a true man. She remembered Ollie. He was a boy, a lad, distinguished by a mental defect she didn't understand. James was sincere. He treated her with respect and enjoyed her mental acuity. He praised her beauty in so many ways she appreciated. He respected her family and friends in a way no other man she knew did. The old cliche "salt of the earth" resonated. He certainly showed that. She loved him. She knew she had made a good decision; she thought about how their children would grow strong and connect with the sea in their own way. She wanted him, and she knew he wanted her. They were a good match. She decided to join him on the warm sand.

Walking hand in hand, she said to him, "This is a wonderful place. So serene. I could spend the rest of my life here."

He answered, "Until real life steps in for us."

"What a wonderful life it will be."

In the mid-afternoon, they stopped in for a quick lunch at the pavilion. Holding her against the wooden railing, he kissed her. She kissed back, aroused, then buried her face in his chest. "Let's go," he said. "We should pack and get ready to go back to Columbia."

Once inside the beach house, he held her again and kissed her. They reached the bed, and he sat on the edge. He pulled her onto his lap where she felt his hardness against her thigh.

"Lie down here." He slid down his bathing trunks.

"Oh, my, the purple volcano." She kissed him on his cheek and mouth and opened her lips to his tongue. Her hand circling his hardness, she circled his ear with her tongue. His heart thumping wildly, he erupted almost immediately, her hand warm and wet between the fingers. "Ah, what a strong thing you are."

born again

Always exhausted. Always wet. Always scared. The price we paid for defending Vietnam, The Republic of. Barbaric warriors with not much purpose. We gathered in groups near the river. "Why are we even here?" groused Lee. "The other side of the world, not appreciated, left to our own devices for survival."

"Survival only," said McKenzie. "That's all we have."

Sam said to Bernie, sweat dripping off his chin, "What do you think? You're new here."

"I don't know. I don't care. I just want to do some good."

"Then, maybe you'd like to join me on medcap." Joyner brightened. "I'd like that."

Sam warned, "Just remember you're an infantryman. You're paid to do a job."

His brown eyes fell. "Yes, sir."

"Turner's worried about the recent ambushes down the river. So far, we've lost three men. He wants us to do a special 'bush tonight."

"What's so special about it, Lieutenant?" I asked.

"You'll walk to the site before dusk."

"That's unique."

"Shea, Flaherty, Lee, Rickie-Bear, Metger on 79, Sergeants. Egan and McKenzie and grenadier Smitty. You'll leave at fifteen hundred hours."

We walked past the village over a network of berms. We reached some woods with a dry path leading across a small stream, then onto a dry trail. Two wood lines later, the ground opened onto a field to our ambush site. We had time before dark, and set up to wait. I asked Ardal, "Do you have a girlfriend in Ireland?"

"Philadelphia."

"Irish-American?"

"Italian."

They shared details about different girls back home and things they hoped to do with them.

"So, Shea," Lee said, "I heard those Italian girls give great blow-jobs. Licking like it was an ice cream cone."

"Stop it!" Smitty barked. "You're givin' me a hard on." Ardal blushed.

Smitty rolled on his side and unbuttoned his jungle pants. We watched him throttle and groan.

"Hey Smitty," Ardal called. "Ye chokin' the chicken, are ye."

When Smitty finished, he buttoned back and sighed. "That's better."

"Let's face it," Rickie-Bear said. "We all need a woman."

"Yeah," Lee said. "The village girls are looking better and better."

"But we can't get to 'em," said Rickie-Bear.

Ardal winked at me, and I nodded back. We fell silent and moved to a straight line near the river. A confluence of two large canals passed a rice field. We spread out about ten meters apart and waited for the night. Rain began to fall intermittently from light to moderate. We watched the pale horizon above the canal's flow and decided on a two-man watch through the night. It might be a long one.

But just before dusk, McKenzie whispered, "Hey. Look over there."

We saw VC forming in the rice paddy; there must've been fifty of them.

"And look there." He pointed down the canal at a sampan loaded with more for crossing. Ardal and I, on the left flank, saw two sampans ferrying black-clad guerrillas. Now there were some seventy to eighty enemy gathering.

McKenzie jumped to the radio. "Six, this is three-three, Salem, fire for effect."

The artillery came smashing in. We opened fire with everything we had. Ardal and I concentrated our fire on the sampan; VC jumped into the water and became easy targets. The machine guns mowed down the enemy in the rice field. Those that hadn't been dropped by artillery scrambled on their hands and knees, dragging their dead and wounded. We went on a line and chased the rest toward the river, like drunken soldiers screaming the rebel yell. "We got 'em!" Egan cried. "Caught 'em cold!"

Payback released all our vengeance and frustration. Not a shot fired back; the artillery was called off; we wanted to cross the water and continue, but the canal presented too much of a barrier. "Cease fire! They're gone."

A time for trembling. We had spent fifteen minutes of fury and were shaken from the result. No casualties. No crying. Just the pure satisfaction of victory. "Whatta we do now?" someone asked. "Body count?"

Rickie-Bear answered, "There won't be any to count. As always, only blood."

"Sit tight," Egan said. "Try to get some sleep and move out in the morning."

* * *

Conquering heroes, we were welcomed back the next day. Sam grinned, "My little Rangers! I'm so proud. That's what you are—Rangers! All of you."

Captain Turner came by. "Good work, men. We've put a serious dent into their operations here; the ambushes will end." He had engineered the mission, but he gave us the credit. "You men will have the night off. Rest and enjoy yourselves. Tomorrow afternoon we have a company in AO Mary. I'm proud of you."

We lounged in front of the tent, going over the day before. "We didn't have a single casualty." McKenzie nodded all around. "We caught them by surprise."

Bernie, who had taken it all in, reflected, "They were still human beings. They had families and aspirations. They were fighting for their homes and country against invaders."

"Go 'head, put a damper on our efforts, Bernie." It was Lee. "We're trying to survive, and you're making it sound like murder."

"I'm human."

"Sounds to me," Ardal said. "You're putting yourself above us. You think you're better?"

Lee then said, "You know, I've been thinking hard about all this.

I've developed a theory: It seems to me that we've been placed in a dilemma; we feel like victims being sent here, and we're left with survival instincts. That's turned us into cold blooded killers."

"That's pretty heavy," I answered, "but you make sense."

Bernie continued, "I just don't believe it all now. I'll still do what I'm trained to do, but I do question this mission.

With that, we fell into a calm. "A night off," I said. "What will we do?"

"Just like the captain said. Rest for tomorrow's mission in Mary."

"AO Mary," McKenzie said. "It oughta be a cakewalk."

Ardal asked, "What's this AO all about?"

"Only the mildest of them all," I answered. "Hard ground, fewer canals to cross, and not much enemy. Maybe a few snipers."

"That's a relief."

The next day I needed to see Co Hue. It was mid-morning, and her family would be out in the rice fields.

I found her sweeping the clay front yard. Her eyes sparkled when she saw me; she made a quick nod toward the door, and we went in. Without the usual pleasantries, I pulled off her white pajamas and pushed her onto the mat. She uttered a grunt and opened her legs, but questioned me with her eyes. I forced myself into her and made a savage thrust so hard she grunted and moaned. A final push and the hot thickness came. Only minutes later, a second time, more violent, more punishing than the first. I felt like a barbarian plundering the village. Sated, I watched her tear up with a hurt look. I was ready to move on to the next village; take another, maybe more women at my mercy. I dressed, but she didn't look at me, and she lay back down on the mat as I left.

I returned to the river where Ardal, McKenzie, and I shared a joint. As the smoke calmed our nerves, I shared, "Time for my nap."

Ardal leaned over. "I think I'm going to visit Hue. Do you think her family's still out in the fields?"

"Yes. And please, be gentle with her."

That afternoon heavy clouds rolled in, but our mission was not called off. As predicted, AO Mary received us calmly. Since the lifts would be an hour apart, we easily set up a perimeter and waited as it began to rain. It soon drove hard. Nipa palm bent under it, and snowy egrets slumped like wet linen on a laundry line. Coconut palm still stood tall, appearing as palace guards against fluvial invasion. We covered ourselves with ponchos—hoods over our heads and beneath our helmets. Raindrops blurred our vision. We had to constantly wipe our eyes to see. From a perimeter, we became a clump.

"You heavens above," Joyner said. "Rain down my righteousness; let the clouds shower it down. Let the earth open wide, let salvation spring up, let righteousness flourish with it; I, the LORD, have created it. Isaiah 45:8."

"Doc. You know there's no hope for us. Psalms, yea, though we walk through the valley of the shadow of death, we will fear nothing. For we are the evil!"

"That's right," Rickie-Bear cried out. "Don't mean nothin.' Not a thing, not a thing."

Joyner replied, "We will all meet our maker."

The second lift came in. We spread our perimeter, and covered our weapons under the ponchos. With the driving rain, the hard packed mud became soggy until it turned into a bog. The egrets lifted heavily and flew in wide circles.

"We haven't heard the first shot," Rickie-bear said, smiling.

"A cakewalk," remarked McKenzie. "Why don't we just call it quits and get back to the village?"

Ardal chimed in, "Better things are waiting for us there." He winked at me.

The third lift disembarked, and we made a line. Our platoon was sent forward a bit to anchor the right flank. On the captain's order, we moved out and carried our weapons still under our ponchos. The unrelenting rain pounded us, dripping from our helmets, and fogging our vision. As we moved close to the Go Cong River, we paused. Turner said, "I don't think we have to go any further. It's clear. Call in the choppers; set up chalks, and let's get out of here."

Rickie-Bear, for some reason, drifted closer to the bank. He saw a big, sea-worthy sampan chugging downstream. He raised his hands and called out, "*Lai dei*, mother fucker!"

"Get back here," Sam yelled. "We're gettin' ready to pull out."

With his arms still raised, a fifty caliber machine gun opened up with a short burst. Rickie was lifted off the ground and nearly cut in half. "No! No! Not Rickie-Bear!"

The engine rumbled louder as the boat picked up speed, leaving a wake behind.

"Rickie-Bear," cried Lee. "Rickie-Bear!"

"It's no use," Sam said. "He's gone. Let's go get him."

Rickie-Bear's lifeless body lay in two parts. Rivulets of rain and blood ran off the mounds of flesh and fatigues. They reached him and, awestruck, quickly turned away.

"Not Rickie-Bear," Sam cried, "What are we going to do without him? He's our soul. Our defender. Our most powerful weapon!" Sam broke down.

Lee dropped to his knees and sank inches in the mud. He searched the sky with his fists to his face. "When is it ever gonna end? God help us!"

"Lieutenant," Turner barked, "tend to your men. You still have a job to do."

"Ready?"

"All set," said Bernadette.

"Then, let's go."

She raised her arm and pointed. "Straightaway!"

They drove onto I-77 northward to Charlotte. Bernadette said, "I still don't see how you can drive on the wrong side of the road."

"Honey. The whole world does."

"We don't."

"Because you're Irish, and the Irish have a way of doing things different."

They drove through the counties: Fairfield, Chester, the edge of Lancaster, then York.

Entering Rock Hill, Jimmy slowed down. "Speed trap," he explained.

"But there's carts passing us."

"Maybe they can afford the fine. Or maybe they're in a big hurry."

"I don't think I'll ever understand driving here."

Down the hill from York, they crossed the Catawba River into North Carolina. She read the state motto sign: Esse Quad

Videri. "That's interesting. To be rather than to seem. Does every state have a motto?"

"Yes."

Once past Charlotte, they entered Iredell County.

"This is one of those counties that's similar in size to Irish counties. We'll go a long way before the next one."

Reaching into the countryside after passing Statesville, the landscape presented green and brown rolling hills and tobacco, corn, hog farms, and some vineyards. She shifted in her seat and pulled the hem of her shorts straight.

Turning to the window, "So beautiful," she said. "So expansive. I like the clouds. Light and fluffy, like cotton balls. What's that mountain over there? It's rising out of nowhere and stands alone."

"Wait until we climb the mountain in Virginia," Jimmy said. "You'll get a better view of it. It's called Mount Pilot. That reminds me. Are you ready for a stop? It'll be a good place before we go up the mountain." He exited the highway and entered a Sheetz store car park.

After the rest room, they bought hot dogs, potato chips, and a Coke, then sat on the patio to eat and rest.

James said, "I like your friends Harper, Ellsbeth, and Caroline. "Could you share with me?"

"I love them. I met Caroline at hospital. I was very sick, and she worked in the emergency room. I liked her right off."

"What about Harper?"

"She's a hairdresser. I met her in the village. She's good."

"Are they from Dunmore East?"

"Harper is. Caroline is from Wexford. Ellsbeth grew up in Bray before she moved to Waterford. She's in insurance."

Some road workers passed by with their lunch. "What's that thing on a stick? It looks like it might be a hotdog."

"Corndog; covered with cornmeal batter and deep fried. Wanna try one?"

"I'd rather have a bun." She used her napkin to wipe his face. "Ketchup."

Back on the road, they crossed the state line. "Virginia Is For Lovers."

"We're lovers." She grinned. "Grand motto."

"We climb this hill until we reach a plateau."

She saw Mount Pilot again. "Like a bald man with a toupee standing erect from the plains."

"I call it the Tower of Piso."

"That's Italy."

"Italy. It's Tower of Pisa. Here it's Piso. Erect like a man."

She gently slapped his arm.

"What are those steep, dirt roads across the highway?" She was looking back at the downhill lanes.

"Escape ramps for runaway trucks. Sometimes a tractor-trailer will lose its brakes; the ramps are there for them to stop in case of emergency."

"You Yankees think of everything."

"Experience."

I-77 guided them through two long tunnels until they reached the West Virginia line: Wild Wonderful West Virginia.

"And "Country Roads," that's a wonderful song. Thinking of songs, Jimmy, do you remember that one we danced to at the party?...I think it was "I Can't live Without You.""

"Corny."

"You mean sentimental. I like sentimental songs."

"Like Gaelic love songs? So sad and tragic. You know the poet Edgar Allen Poe? He once said the greatest poetic subject is the death of a beautiful woman."

"As long as it's not mine. But that song. I don't think I could live without you."

"Don't say that. It makes me nervous. Besides, Ardal told me nobody could ever kill me; I've been blessed with God's grace."

She leaned over and kissed his cheek. "I hope so."

"We're going to catch the Mountaineer Expressway up here. It's a scenic drive and a shortcut, as well."

The mountains rose higher. Unlike on the interstate, Jimmy had to negotiate occasional traffic lights. She said, "Those clouds remind of Ireland."

"It does," Jimmy said. "Are you missing home now?"

"A little. But this trip has been so much fun."

"I'm glad, but I can tell you, I'm missing my new home, as well."

They came to a long, arched bridge over the New River Gorge. He drove across, then turned right into a visitors' parking lot. Inside the center, displays hung neatly on stone walls, some exhibits depicting coal mines and railroads. Outside, she found a viewing scope and was turning a couple of knobs.

"Here," he said, "you have to put fifty cents in it."

"Deadly. I can see way afar. Beautiful!"

"Check those oaks over there."

"Poetic."

"C'mon. Let's check the shop across the road, then leave."

She found a rack of sweatshirts with the gorge logo. "I think I'll get these for Caroline, Harper, and me."

"Why don't you get one of these?"

""Paddle faster. I hear banjo music. What's that mean?" She held one over her chest.

"There was a movie back in the seventies where three ad execs from Atlanta went to the mountains for a canoeing weekend. Somebody got raped, and I think another drowned. Just a bad trip all around. And there was a famous scene of banjo playing.

"Ergo, row faster. I hear banjo music."

"I don't think I want to see that movie!"

"It got some kind of award that year."

Bernadette looked at the shirt, then at him. She cracked a smile. "You're a boor."

"Make up your mind on the shirts. We need to get outta here."

"Straightaway, then."

"Keep on truckin.'"

They descended Mount Powell and plunged to the Birch River town. Nine miles later, they hooked onto I-79.

"How far now? It's been a long drive. James, would you really try to do that to me?"

"Why not? You have a great arse."

She pinched his arm. Hard. "You're disgusting, as well!"

He pulled off the road at the next rest stop and wrapped his arms around her. "You shouldn't always take me so seriously." Then he kissed her.

She responded with a twirl. "Let's get back on the road."

"Pennsylvania state motto: Virtue, Liberty, and Independence." She laughed, "You're only two of those!"

They passed the outskirts of Pittsburgh and neared Crafton.

"Okay. This is it. Turn here, and we're only five miles away." He passed several traffic lights and climbed a steep, cobblestone hill.

"Dublin with hills," she remarked.

"We have many cobblestone and brick streets. Here we are, at my old house."

"That's a big house. Was your family rich?"

"Not hardly. It was built in 1870. When my parents bought it, that house needed a lot of fixing. My dad and I did most of it."

"I can see all the places where you told me about playing hide-and-seek!"

"Oh, yeah, sometimes we'd have more than twenty kids playing."

"I don't see," she said, "any fields where you'd play that stick game you told me about."

He pointed, "There."

"Where?"

"On the street corner there. Home plate was that sewer lid on the corner; first, that sewer lid across the street. We used a sidewalk square up the street for second, and the one back across for third."

"Imaginative. Do any of your friends still live around here?"

"One. She still lives two doors up."

"Can we go visit?"

"I haven't seen her in a while. Sure, let's go see her."

At the back door of a small brick house, he knocked lightly. "CALLING ON JJ!"

A woman opened the door. "Jimmy! What a nice surprise! Where have you been?"

"Out of town."

"I remember you told me you were going to Ireland for a golf tournament."

"I stayed on for a few months. I want you to meet my fiancée, Bernadette Bohan."

Her eyes widened. "Fiancée? You finally did it, and I can see why! She's gorgeous."

Bernadette blushed. "I didn't mean to embarrass you," JJ said.

"I'll make some coffee. Here, sit down at the table."

A couple of cats came into the kitchen. One of them jumped on the table. "Get down, Gretchen! Sorry, she loves people."

"So Judy," Jimmy said, "still goin' to Steeler games?"

"Not anymore. It's such a hassle now, with the new stadium. "I have to take the carline down town, then I have to walk across the bridge to get there. Too many jagoffs."

"We're goin' in town for two days before we head back to Ireland."

"You serious about this. You goin' to live there?"

"We've already decided."

"Gawd, Jimmy, you surprise me, but I guess it shouldn't. You always were an adventurer. What's the weather over there?"

"Like this," Bernadette chimed in. "A wee bit cooler."

"Not like that gawd awful heat in South Carolina. You take sugar or cream?'

"Cream, it is."

"I like your accent. Charming."

JJ had a way of talking in almost a sing-song voice. Her real name was Judy Jessep, one of the neighborhood kids he had grown up with.

"Where in Ireland?"

"Waterford," James said. "A small village called Dunmore East."

"That where you goin' to settle?"

"Dingle," Bernadette corrected. "We're going to live in Dingle. That's on a peninsula in the far west."

"Very nice. I'm gonna miss ya, Jimmy."

"You can always visit."

"Too many animals to take care of. I can't get away, you know that."

"How are they doin,' by the way?"

"The groundhogs under the front porch had little ones; there's five of them now. And the raccoons added one; three of them now."

"Are you still feeding them out in the corner?"

"No. They come to the back porch nah. Keepin' up with food around here's becoming a chore."

"Expensive, too, I imagine."

"Yeah, well, I love my pets. I have to take care of them. As long as they hang around, I have to take care of them, y'know."

"Aren't they wild animals?" Bernadette asked.

"We have a herd of deer comin' around lately, too. Gawd. It's like a nature preserve now." She chuckled. "I have some chipped ham, if you'ns hungry. How long was the trip?"

"Have you seen Ding-Dong lately?"

"Gawd, no, thank goodness. But the Wiggy boys still live in the neighborhood."

"Really?"

"Big Wiggy is in bad shape. He's bedridden now with Parkinson's. A burden on his wife."

"What about Little Wiggy?"

"He cuts my yard about once a month. We go out with some of his friends. Mostly lunch. Can I fix you a sandwich?"

"We have to leave soon. I want to get there before dark."

"Where are you stayin'?"

"The William Penn."

"That's pretty fancy now. A big hotel chain bought it out."

"I didn't know that. It seemed reasonable."

"Are you takin' Bernadette through the Tube?"

"Tube, is it?" Bernadette asked.

"Oh, I like her," JJ said. "It's the accent."

"Well, thanks, Judy. We better go now. Sorry for the short visit."

"Thanks for stoppin' by. I'm so glad to meet your fiancée." She turned to Bernadette. "Y'know, girls used to swarm around him in high school. You're the lucky girl."

Bernadette smiled. "I know."

He drove past the high school. "This is where we went to intermediate."

"Looks like a castle."

"It is. English castle. See the towers. They were for the music classes. The dungeon had the cafeteria and swimming pool. There's a courtyard in the middle. What do you think?"

"Needs a feckin' moat."

"I guess they didn't have enough room. It was built on a vineyard."

He guided the car past the train station, up the Berry Street hill, then steered over to Noblestown Road. He crossed over Greentree to catch I-379. "This is the Tube coming up."

"O mo dia! It's a tunnel!"

Through the Tube, the breathtaking view of downtown Pittsburgh, she said, "Oh! It's spectacular! I see the road lights flickering from the river. And those tall buildings, and so many bridges! What's that tall one with the orange top?"

"The Gulf Building. Orange means fair and warm weather; if it blinks, it'll be inclement."

They reached the William Penn on Grant Street as light was fading. The valet parked the car, and they checked in. Just seven stories tall, the hotel seemed old fashioned.

"A king bed," exclaimed Bernadette. "Just like your room at home."

He asked, "You want something to eat or go to sleep?"

"Sleep. I can eat tomorrow."

They undressed and slipped under the covers.

She said, "You're not going to swell again, are you?"

"Too tired."

After sleeping soundly and waking late next morning, they dressed and just had a coffee.

"It's almost lunch," Jimmy said. "I think we should go shopping for an outfit for tonight's dinner. First, I want to take you for a special sandwich."

He took her down Fourth Avenue, where the brownstone and tall gray buildings lined the street. He found a lunch counter. "Try this," he said. "It's a Pittsburgh original, the Turkey Devonshire." He ordered one each, and a side of fries. The sandwich was open-faced with shaved turkey breast covered with slices of tomato and bacon and a smooth, thin cheese sauce ribboned across.

"Good," said Bernadette with a full mouth. "I'm famished, and this is great." She sipped on her Pepsi. "You said shopping. I love sending messages!"

"You need to go to Western Union?"

"Why?"

"To send a message home?"

She smiled. "It means shopping. I love the goo."

"I can buy you some caramel fudge, if you like gooey stuff."

She rolled her eyes.

The boutique offered fine, expensive women's outfits. The sales lady fawned over Bernadette. He sat on a cushioned chair and watched the process; he loved shopping with women, seeing the different outfits, and being asked the comparatives. He watched her full body turning side to side, and the frequent glances in the mirror. She would open her arms and model. He liked everything she tried on.

She made her choice with a look of satisfaction. "What do you think?"

"I think every man in the city's goin' to love it."

She winked. "Can you wrap and box it, please? And thank you so much."

"Let's get a beer at the hotel."

They returned and dropped off her purchases in the room. "What are you going to wear tonight, James?"

"Oh, I have a suit just for the occasion. A blue cord."

"I can't wait to see you in it."

* * *

The bar was quiet before the usual crowd came in. "Two Irons," James ordered.

The bartender slid the drafts before them. Bernadette raised her glass and inspected. "Nice body. I like the collar; it seals the flavor." She took a sip. "Good."

"That's what I like to see," the bartender said. "Someone who knows how to drink a good beer."

"She should," James said. "She's Irish."

"Okay. You two married?"

"Engaged."

"You Irish, too?"

"Workin' on it."

"I must say. A fine looking couple. She's Irish, and you're American. Wowser, wow-wow-wowser!"

"You sound like Frank Sinatra. You Italian?"

"Very. Drink up. The next one's on me."

"Are you tryin' to con a tip?"

"James." Bernadette nudged him. "Behave."

"That's right," the bartender said. "I'm not tryin' to squeeze ya. They pay me well."

"He didn't mean to say it that way. Sorry."

"Forgiven." He shook their hands and tried to smooch Bernadette. "Another? On me?"

"Oh yes. Thank you."

James left a fifty-dollar tip, and as they left the bar, she squeezed his arm. "Let's make tonight special. It'll be our last night in the States. I've had a grand time. I want this memory to last forever."

They dressed for dinner. She wore her new cocktail dress: navy blue, split in back at the knee; black nylons; and the black silk wrap to offset her ruby earrings. The color contrast lent a special glow to her hair and eyes. He put on his blue cord suit with a blue striped bowtie.

"How do I look?" he beamed.

"Here, let me help you. Your tie's crooked, and you missed a button on your coat." She attended. "And look at your hair! Don't you ever brush and comb?"

"I use my fingers."

"Okay, I'll straighten it for you. You could use a haircut."

"I like my hair the way it is."

She sighed. "There. You look handsome now. Shall we go?"

"Haircut, is it? Straightaway."

The concierge hailed a cab for them and waved, "What a good looking couple! Enjoy your evening."

"Incline," James told the driver.

She said, "Incline?"

"It's a rail car used to climb the steep hill to Mount Washington. It could fit twenty-five passengers, but a few would have to stand." Tourists were already waiting at the brick station, hoping to catch the first available. James and Bernadette missed the first two trips, but the car from the top descended while the station car ascended, and they caught the third one.

She gripped both James and the wooden arm in the rail car. "I think I left my stomach at the bottom."

"Don't worry. It's perfectly safe." At the top James offered his wing, and they walked a couple hundred yards to the Lamont restaurant.

She said, "I remember when you did this on the way home from disco. That was the first time I touched you."

"I remember very well. That turned out to be a special night for us."

They entered the Lamont. A warm ambience greeted them; soft, low lights and deep carpeting. They were directed to a table close to the large bay window, where they could see over the city below.

"See," she said, "the street lights dance across the river. And so many bridges!"

"Beautiful view," James returned. "Three rivers needed the bridges. See, there's the Fort Pitt Bridge, the Northside Bridge from Sixth Street, and two more up river. That's the Allegheny. Below is the Monongahela River."

The waiter, dressed in classical black and white, with an apron reaching almost to his ankles, asked, "Can I get you something to drink, an appetizer?"

Before James could speak, she said to the waiter, "We'd like *charcuterie au fromage. Kirsch, Brie, et Camembert.*"

The waiter retreated. The maître d' appeared for the order. "*A votre service.*"

"*Oui. Craquelins palets bretons, petite beurre,* and *lunette de romans.*"

"*Vins?*"

"*Oui. Chateau Phillipe-Le-Hardi.* Oh. *Et chateau de brand mi-saignant.*"

"*Oui, Madame.*"

James said, "French, too? What did you say?"

"We're having tenderloin and Burgundy wine. I thought you'd like that."

He saw her in a new light—confidence, self-assured, present. *Damn, am I lucky to have found her. She radiates. I now realize how truly lost I've been. The only structure in my life had been the military and the church. I'd been drifting so many years, and now, because of her, I've found a new purpose.*

The wine came. The maître d' poured for her to taste.

She swirled her glass, placed it under her nose, and after a small taste, said, "Berries, especially raspberry; a certain redolence—rosemary perhaps." She looked at the maître d' and nodded approval.

He poured for both.

They relished the charcuterie.

James said, "You shock me sometimes."

She raised her glass and smiled. "To us."

"May we live forever."

"Do you like dogs?" she asked.

"Oh yeah. When we move to Dingle, I'd like a border collie or two."

She smiled after another swallow. "We'll need plenty of land, then. Better to have two of them so they can play together."

"And with our kids."

James saw a string quartet in tuxedos setting up.

The chateau arrived, and the maître d' carefully sliced and served them. "I hope,"

She said, "You like medium rare."

A colorful array of vegetables accompanied. "*Pommes Parisienne*!" she exulted.

They silently feasted while the quartet played a mixture of classical and contemporary songs. "So charming. Thank you for bringing me here, James. This is our last night in the States, and you've made it so memorable. Thank you, my heart."

James saw a well-coiffed gentleman approach the quartet; probably making a request, he guessed. They continued with classical tunes before a short break. He and Bernadette enjoyed with slow, measured bites the meal, then James poured another glass for them. "Uh-oh. Looks like the last of it."

"Would you like me to order another?"

"I don't know. It might be too much."

"On a special occasion like this. Where's your spirit?"

She called the waiter back. "*Garçon. Vin Rose de Tavel.*"

"*Oui, Madame.*"

They drank and savored the pink wine. Their eyes fixed on one another. They raised their glasses for another toast. The quartet resumed their play. They went into "Magic Moment," and he saw her smile. "Shall we?"

Others went onto the dance floor—at least eight or ten couples. James and Bernadette rose and glided into their dance cheek-to-cheek. "I love our song," she said. "Such pleasant memories." His lips on her cheek, he held her closer and murmured, "I love you, Bernadette Caitlin Flaherty."

Now hazy-eyed, they prepared to end the evening. "*J'ai apprecicie mon repas,*" she told the maître d.' "*Merci, Madame. Repete.*"

Back in their room, only one lamp was on. They stood near the bed and embraced. She rose on her toes and passionately kissed him. She stepped back and undid his bowtie then removed his jacket. She slowly unbuttoned his shirt and rested her head on his chest, feeling the soft hair against her cheek and breathing in his scent. She unzipped his trousers and let them slide to the floor, and with one hand, eased him onto the bed. Lying next to him, she listened to his heartbeat, which quickened as did hers. The hair on his arm was soft as she stroked and moved down, exploring his thighs; his calves. Her eyes were fixed on his body as she stepped away and undressed. Slowly.

He saw her white breasts contrast with her tanned arms and legs. Her nipples, dark cherry, stood erect. As she moved toward him, he could see the golden softness in the shadow of her tanned belly. She slid onto the bed next to him and cupped his face with her hand, her nipples brushing his skin. Their lips hard together, they eagerly sought with their tongues. He rose onto his knees and began kissing her legs, her calves, and her thighs. In the pale skin below her navel, he licked and smelled her.

She moaned and arched her back. "Jimmy, now," she gasped.

His penis throbbing, he pushed between the moist folds and entered her. He kissed her forehead and cheeks, her lips, and their tongues danced. Feeling each other's hot breath, their hips moved together, his strokes faster for a final, deep thrust. He ejaculated wet and hot. She felt his heat inside her as they lay still, breaths slowing. "What a lovely ride," she whispered. "We're meant for one another."

"I look forward to our life together," James said.

She rose on her elbow. "My heart is within you."

Next morning, they packed, checked out, and drove to the airport. While waiting for their flight, she said, "James. What are you going to do with all that money?"

"Deposit in a local bank; maybe three accounts, one for investing."

She put her left arm around his shoulder and placed her right hand in his lap. "May I ask you a question? What the feck is a jagoff?"

"A most annoying person."

She kissed his cheek. "I'm glad you're not a jagoff, but ye sure did talk funny back there."

"Bang on."

Bernie found village medcap fulfilling. He liked dealing with the kids and helping Joyner tend to poisonous bites, boils, cuts, and scratches. Doc could administer penicillin if required. Together, they worked diligently. The villagers respected them so much, they even invited them to go to the Ong Ke Khiem's home. The most venerable lived in the hamlet across the bridge. He was considered the village's wisest; the one who settled disputes and family problems. Most importantly, the people visited him for his geomancy predictions, to decide propitiousness. He could read the lunar signs by the second, minute, hour, day, month, and year to admonish for trips, weddings, and even birth. His house was full of gifts, and he didn't charge for any service provided. Women came to clean his house, tend to his garden, and even bathe him. The Ong Ke Khiem was considered the precious one.

He had a growth on his neck that needed tending. Doc saw that he would have to lance and disinfect the area. After he successfully did so, villagers began bringing Doc and Bernie special things, like food, sewing, limes for their skin, and sometimes *bao se dai*, a potent rice wine used for celebrations. One day, a teenager came with a bite from a viper. Joyner was back at the platoon area, so Bernie lanced the wound himself and put some salve on it. Joyner would've called for a dust off to airlift the boy back to Battalion aid, where they kept a stock of anti-venom. The next day, a little girl came in a panic. Bernie rushed to the thatched house and found the boy writhing with sweats and fever. He repeated the disinfecting and rewrapped the bandage. He waited all afternoon with the family until the kid stopped shaking and began smiling and joking. So stunned were the villagers, they began to call Bernie the *bac si*, the medicine man. Joyner and Bernie later learned the nearest *bac si* was four villages away to the north.

Joyner still scolded Bernie, "You might've killed that boy! Don't ever do that again."

Bernie smiled and said softly, "I won't." But the villagers treated the new soldier with reverence.

Bernie and Joyner took the rice liquor to the platoon for anyone who wanted to drink it during off hours. Joyner then approached Lieutenant Sam again, asking that Bernie be taken off line.

"He's too valuable on medcap. I'd hate to lose him in the field."

Sam pondered and turned all the possibilities over but told Doc, "I can't do that."

"Why?"

"As platoon leader, I'm responsible for all the men. It wouldn't be fair to them. And we need all the men we can muster."

"But I was just issued a Car-15, so I'm armed now, and another combat-ready troop has been added."

"Doc. Do you think you're actually going to use that rifle? I can't take that chance. The Army should've trained Bernie for the Medical Corp."

"Or a chaplain's assistant."

Sam said, "We have a platoon mission tomorrow, and I don't know what it's all about. Some kind of secret they won't tell me. Sorry, Thomas, Bernie's going to have to go with us."

"Roger-Dodger. Maybe if we get more replacements, you could reassign him."

"Maybe. I don't know."

* * *

I lit up a "j" "Hey, Ardal," I said. "What do you think about the new guy?"

"Bernie seems alright, He's a bit annoying, always wanting to help. Y'notice how he's always saying, 'May I help you?' It's gettin' on my nerves. He needs to help himself."

"Yeah. He has to learn if he wants to survive. I can't figure him out."

Passing the joint back and forth, we thought about the upcoming mission on the scuttlebutt; we had heard the Rung Sat. I said to Ardal, "I always hated that place. Mangroves with too many oddball creatures. Hell, the fuckin' bees are bigger than my hand."

"Lot of enemy?"

"I can't figure that place out, either. We don't get hit much there. I know the place is swarming with Charlies, but they leave us alone so far."

"Do you know what strength we'll have?"

"We only go in small groups. Platoon or twelve men. And we can't stay there more than one night."

"Are we doin' an overnight?"

"I hope not. The tide keeps the place wet. Remember to bring your hammock. We have to sleep in the trees."

Sam and Joyner came upon us. Doc now carried his Car-15 strapped over his shoulder. The smaller version of the 16 looked like a toy, and on Doc, a comic look.

"Are you gonna shoot that thing, Thomas?"

Ardal and I had the giggles.

"Only for defense," Doc said.

The Lieutenant said, "Listen up. Thirteen of us are going to the Rung Sat tomorrow. Leave very early in the morning, so it will be a day mission."

"What the fuck, over!" Peter yelled, "I have to carry the damn radio in that fuckin' swamp!"

"Want me to carry it for you?" Lee razzed. "I can strap it over my sixty. Seventy pounds, no sweat."

"Fuck you, Lee!"

"We'll have to go light," I said. "One C box, one canteen."

"Pass it on," Sam said. "Oh six hundred."

"Let's do another," Ardal said. "I want to swim in my mind."

"The rains have let up," I returned. "Maybe we can trip on the moon tonight."

* * *

We linked on the road for the four choppers to pick us up. A group mission borrowed men from the other two platoons. We carried most of the load. Andy, Matt, and a new guy named Phil would join us. We set up chalks for the birds and waited. We had Lee, Peter, Ardal, myself, Lorenzo, Metgar, McKenzie, Thomas Joyner, and Bernie. Lieutenant Sam, of course, would lead us on the mysterious mission.

The helicopters banked onto the dirt road and picked us up. We would fly at least an hour. The choppers had to land an LZ a mile from the Rung Sat. Across the sea-worthy Dong Nai River, we would bank onto the LZ.

"Six. This is three-six oscar. Cold LZ."

"Three-six oscar, this is six oscar. Roger. Stay alert. CC's coming."

We marched in columns. Sam took point; Ardal and I pulled slack, and Metgar with his grenade launcher (loaded with a canister round) went flank. Andy from the other platoon picked up the left flank. We moved forward in a light drizzle. Further on, the ground became softer. The rotten swamp roots oozed a most foul smell, as if a black pall blended with the darkness of the forest. On and on we went until Sam stopped us for a short break.

Lee groused, "I hate this place."

"I'd take Liza over this," McKenzie returned.

"I never saw anything like this," Ardal said. "It's so dark and gloomy. Makes my skin crawl."

"That's right, Irishman. Roll down your sleeves and cover your head with your jungle hat." Andy spoke with a nervous jitter.

After an hour of slogging, we came to our rendezvous spot. "What time is it?" I asked.

"Thirteen hundred hours," Sam called. "Let's set up near the bank and wait. For what, I don't know. Following instructions."

McKenzie rummaged through his pack. "Damn! I forgot my hammock."

"You can use mine," Bernie offered.

McKenzie cried, "Bernie, you're crazy! You don't know what it's like out here."

"But we're not staying the night. I can manage."

"I wish I had a joint," Ardal said.

"Not here," McKenzie answered. "When we get back in the 'ville."

We closed together in the dank air. We found a seat wherever we could find some suitable ground. A couple of orange snakes hung from the trees, and giant hornets buzzed around the tops of bushes. The tide lapped away. Just then, a huge lizard rose from the dark water.

"Damn," Lee said, "that thing is huge."

Its leathery head streamed water and strands of slime before Doc fired his Car-15 at it. "Snap! Snap!"

"A salty! Get away!" The crocodile splashed back amid roiling mud.

"Jeezus! That thing could've swallowed us whole."

Lorenzo fired off. "What the fuck, over! Let's get this over with and get out of this hell."

A calm settled in. The rain stopped, but the air didn't grow any lighter. They heard snapping in a clearing. "Whoa! Look at that," Lorenzo pointed.

"A cobra and a mongoose," Lee hissed.

They watched the mongoose dance and leap around the snake. The cobra raised to strike but was too slow to hit the mark. The mongoose circled the reptile.

"Can cobras see out of the back of their heads?" Lorenzo asked.

Joyner, with his biology degree, answered, "Course not. That's part of the mongoose's strategy."

The animals continued their battle lock. The mongoose let out a low 'chitter,' while the snake desperately struck and missed. For more than thirty minutes, the soldiers watched the struggle. The cobra seemed to tire and waver, then the mongoose rushed in and seized the snake by the neck, flipping it back and forth till dead.

"It's like us against Charlie," Phil said. "Despite all our modern weaponry, Sir Charles dances around us, and we can't do shit, the fuckin' little, zipper-headed bastard."

"Let's eat while we're waiting," the Lt said.

"I don't really feel hungry," Ardal said.

"Me neither," I answered. "Anybody else?"

"How can I eat surrounded by this shit?" McKenzie blurted.

Then Bernie said, "Hey guys. I have something for us." He pulled a bottle of wine from his pack and held it over his head, "God's venom."

I said, "Shi-i-i-t! There's not enough wine in that bottle for all of us."

"A taste then. Enough to calm our nerves. How about it?"

"Where did you ever get that?"

"I traded for it." Bernie beamed.

"Traded with who?"

"Sergeant Shoemaker over in second platoon."

Andy barked, "That crazy bastard? A real gaping asshole!"

"Three-six, this is six oscar; commo check, how hear?"

Peter picked up the horn: "Lima-Charlie, Ho Chi Minh, rat-a-tat-tat, hotel-mike."

"Same-same. Six oscar, out."

"Okay, what did you trade?"

"Peaches."

In unison, "PEACHES! You traded peaches with that crazy ass?"

"You haven't been here long enough to store them up!"

Bernie answered, "That was simple. I promised Shoemaker all the peaches I'd get in the next three months."

"Jesus, Bernie. He got over on you big time."

"You don't think it's a fair deal? I think it is. I don't eat peaches."

"We do, asshole. Eat the hell out of them."

"What's the use?" Sam said. "Get out your canteen cups."

They put their cups together, and someone had stale crackers to add.

Bernie poured into their waiting cups. Each soldier couldn't have gotten more than a half ounce. They each took a few crackers and sniffed the wine down.

"Ugh. That's terrible. What the hell is it?"

"Don't worry, guys. It's kosher."

"Oh, so that makes it better?"

"Worst wine I ever tasted," Sam said. "Okay. Stay alert. It should be close to time, for whatever it's going to be."

Sam kept checking his watch, and nervously fidgeted. He finally said, "Okay, troops, it wouldn't be fair to keep you any longer. I'm calling for pickup. Peter, give me the horn." Just then, the brackish water bubbled slightly. They saw two dark and dripping human figures rise and slog ashore.

They unzipped and peeled off wet suits, tossed aside flippers, and drew out tiger fatigues and jungle boots. They produced 9-millimeter submachine guns and attached silencers. One of them waved and said, "Thank you!" and they disappeared into the darkness.

"Far out!"

"Fuck, man." Someone let out a long breath.

"So that's what this is all about—assassins. Let's get to the PZ. Half a click, northwest."

They gathered up their gear, saddled up, and moved out. Peter tossed the empty wine bottle into the water, "So long."

It was always easier to come back than going out. The darkness lightened as they moved on, toward thin streams of sunlight. They slogged out of the stinking, black-rooted muck until they found solid ground.

"There," Sam pointed. He checked his compass, then his watch. "There's our PZ. Just five hundred yards. Peter, call CP for extraction."

Bernie drifted ahead of the group. He seemed to be looking at the ground. Remembering Ricki-Bear, Sam called out: "Come back here, Bernie! What do you think you're doing?"

He didn't look back but kept going at a leisurely pace.

McKenzie called: "Private Bernstein! Stop!"

Metgar said, "He must be roaming the wilderness."

"Somebody go get him!"

"You go out there! You run down that crazy fucker!"

A single shot cracked. Everybody dove to the ground and quickly raised their weapons for return fire, but there was nothing to shoot at.

"Goddammit!"

Doc heard a low moan. "Bernie!" he cried. "It's Bernie."

Ardal, Joyner, and I ran as fast as we could, our packs rattling.

When we reached him, Bernie lay on his side. Faint rays of light shone on the body. All we could do was stare.

Metgar squinted into the sun. "There she goes! See that sniper. She's runnin' away!" He launched a grenade, but it hit a tangle of branches, which made it explode prematurely.

Joyner tried to unload with his new carbine, but the sniper was already gone. "Damn that bitch!"

We all gathered around the body. Sam said, "We can't call in a dust off. We'll have to load him in one of our ships."

"He can go with us," Ardal volunteered.

"Wrap him in a poncho," Sam said. "We'll lay him out across the floor boards."

The choppers dropped us off on the village road then rose and flew off with Bernie's body. We watched dumbly as the bird ascended through the clouds. We were numbed. How did it all happen? What was he thinking? Poor Bernie. It was almost like he was making some sort of sacrifice. It didn't make any sense.

At the platoon, we mourned and replayed Bernie's walk alone into danger. Despite the circumstances, a loss was always heartbreaking. We were getting picked off.

"Damn Vietnam!" It was Lee. "Damned Republic of! Damn green machine! I hate y'all!"

Peter stayed with us. He didn't want to see Shoemaker just yet. "I think I'm going to tear into Shoemaker, that sicko bastard."

"Wait," Joyner countered. "It's not his fault."

"Yeah, but three months of peaches!"

"How many would you draw in three months?"

"I'm lucky if I get three," Ardal said. "Maybe four."

Sam said, "Don't lay it all on Shoemaker. And stop knocking

Bernie. I know he was different, but I liked his attitude. It ended up getting him wasted."

They were quiet for a while before grudgingly agreeing with what the lieutenant said.

"Too nice." McKenzie said. "He was just too nice. That's what made him different. He was always wanting to do good in this stinkin' place. Just a downright good kid."

After listening, I said, "Do you know what we should do? Honor his debt."

"Like a tribute," added Ardal.

"A memoriam," Lee said. "That's it. Memoriam."

"If we expect four draws of peaches a month, we should decide on twelve cans altogether. Agree?"

"Among the twelve of us," Ardal said, "we can do it."

"So let it be done," McKenzie added.

"So I have some good news, guys." Sam smiled. "Our company is scheduled for stand down in two days."

"Do we have shit until then?" Lorenzo asked.

"No," Sam answered. "One day and a wakeup."

From the Dublin Airport, they hauled their bags to Jack's waiting car. "Did you have a good time?"

"Oh yes," Bernadette said. "It was grand."

After negotiating Dublin traffic, past Trinity College, then through Dalkey, Jack drove through open countryside while both travelers dozed. Jack wanted to ask more about their holiday but resigned himself to silence when he saw the sleeping couple.

At Bray, James stirred. "Where are we? I'm anxious to get home."

"Another hour or so. Moira and Harper wanted to come along, but not enough room. Moira has a surprise for you, James. She's so excited about you two; she wanted to share the news with everyone."

Along the way, through the Sun Coast, they reached Wexford. After crossing the River Suir, they turned left into Waterford City, then on to Dunmore East. At the inn, Moira, her husband Tony and Delany greeted them with hugs.

"You're so tanned." Her mother gazed. "The States must've agreed with you."

Bernadette turned and half-posed.

"Let me show you my surprise," Moira said. "Come with me." She led them a short way up the street until they reached a small bungalow. "This is where you're going to live, James." She led the way inside. A narrow, three-room floor plan greeted him. He and his fiancée laughed to see in the main room, only a large bed.

"You remembered!" Bernadette exclaimed.

"I had to get it in Waterford. Like it?"

James said, "Love it. Thanks, Moira."

"You have to establish residence for your application of citizenship."

"You've thought it out," James said. "Thank you, big sister."

The tiny kitchenette sat below a window. "You'll probably want to dine with us at the inn," Moira offered, "but this will do for a quick bite or tea." Then a small bathroom. Moira added, "Small, but with a big enough shower stall for you two. "Here," she handed him an old-fashioned iron key. "This is the only one, so don't lose it. Bernadette, bad news. You're going to have to work tonight."

"Oh, no," she drooped. "Can't you get someone else?"

"Sorry. You better get some winks now." And she gave them both a hug and let herself out the door.

* * *

At six o'clock, Bernadette and James woke in the darkening evening. She sneezed. "You can stay here and sleep while I work."

"Oh no. I want to go, too."

When they entered the inn, they were surprised to see an empty bar and only one light in the dining room. "I wonder what this is all about?"

"Maybe some kind of secret." She raised her eyebrows, "Oh, no, it couldn't be. Come on." The couple was met with bright lights to reveal the extended family and many friends, all smiling.

"G'wan! G'wan! G'wan!" Bernadette cried. "Welcome back!" Harper laughed, giving them a close hug and kiss. "G'wan! G'wan! G'wan! G'wan!!"

"Come in here." Moira waved and led them to a buffet table covered with food, wine, beer, and even a bottle of James' favorite whiskey completed the table.

Copying Bernadette, James cried, "G'wan! G'wan! G'wan!"

Everybody laughed and gathered around them. "Congratulations, James, you did it! The smartest girl in town." It was Aidan from the disco.

Bernadette introduced him to her grandparents, aunts, uncles, and cousins. They were all jovial, and they almost shook his arm away. The grandmothers looked hard at her hand and turned to James: "Where's the ring?"

James blushed. It was something that had never crossed his mind. *How stupid.* "Well...I..."

"We decided it wasn't necessary," Bernadette jumped in. "We love each other as it is."

"But every man expresses his feelings with a ring."

"We decided on claddagh. Means more to us."

Harper, Ellsbeth and Caroline approached James and hugged him. "You've made us so happy! Bernadette talked so much about you when she first met you; we knew then!"

"You've come together," Harper added. "Oh, give us a kiss!"

James and Bernadette managed to get back together. They slipped into the lounge and sat on the sofa. She sneezed again, "I think I might have a bug."

"Maybe it was the weather change—warm in South Carolina, cooler in Pittsburgh, and here, even cooler."

"Perhaps."

Just then Delany and Jack crossed into the lounge from the party. She kissed James, and he closely hugged them both.

"We're so proud. We hope you have a long life and many children." Jack kissed his daughter. "Why don't you two come back to the party?"

"Oh, Daddy, I've caught a bug."

Delany felt Bernadette's forehead. "You have a fever. Let me touch yours, James. No fever. Maybe you won't catch it."

Bernadette looked at James and smiled and half winked.

Moira joined them. "There you are!"

"Your little sister came back from America with the sniffles," Jack said.

"Aww, we'll have to put her in the sick room."

James said, "Well, I'll be staying with her."

They settled her on the big bed in the family sick room. She still was feverish the next morning when Moira brought a light breakfast of honey-lemon tea, brown bread, and orange juice. James was still sitting on the wooden chair at the desk he had used all summer and, for the first time, studied Bernadette's big sister. She always carried a sunny expression, with a ready smile. Her eyes showed love as she cared for her sister. When Bernadette began shivering, Moira also brought her clean pajamas and a heavy quilt. Later that afternoon she brought another pot of tea, urging them to drink. In the evening, James developed a runny nose and started sneezing.

"Twirling," she said and pointed to her lips. "So James, I thoroughly enjoyed our holiday. Thank you."

"I love being with you, too. Now we have the cooties!"

"What a grand time we had." Her voice was raspy. "I liked everything, the beach, the dancing, dinner on top of that high hill. And mostly, our hotel room in Pittsburgh."

"Aye! The hotel. My favorite part." He coughed.

"Do you think we'll go back there again?"

"I don't know. Maybe after we settle in at Dingle."

"I'd like that."

"States or Dingle?"

"Both."

Sneezing, James pointed to the homey Irish quote on the wall. "We should take that down and replace it with a skull and crossbones."

"Oh, surely not."

"I'm gettin' sleepy. I need to lie down. Move over, please." He placed a sheet over the quilt and covered himself with another blanket.

"Remember?" She slid over and rearranged pillows.

"Indeed. The first time we slept together."

"I was so drunk."

"I took your shoes and stockings off. Do you think we should get a ring?" He rose on an elbow and looked into her face.

"A ring is a lovely symbol, but not everyone needs one. I went with Tony when he picked out Moira's ring. He sure had a time trying to choose."

"You're not listening. Could you give me a straight answer?"

"A piece of metal around the finger. Perhaps." She drowsed.

He put his arm around her, and they both fell asleep as darkness fell.

Next morning, Moira brought a small pitcher of orange juice. "Make sure you drink all of this. It'll do ye good." They drank a little and went back to sleep.

"Uh-h-h-h. I feel so bad." He ended up under the quilt with her, shivering. Bernadette's fever had broken, and she was still in bed with James, but she was feeling better.

Moira knocked on the door. "Decent? Lunch time, soup and tea with some fresh cheddar cheese."

"Thanks, but I don't think," Bernadette said, "I can live another day with this tea in it!"

"Relax. Go back to sleep."

In two days, Bernadette was up and felt better. With Moira's care, his recovery would be near. She said, "I have a surprise for you. Harper brought this record and a turntable."

"Our song, so sweet."

"And," Moira continued, "Ollie Savage…Ha!…gave me a message…ha!… for you two."

"Oh. What did he say?" James asked, sitting up in bed.

Big sister returned. "He," Ha-ha-ha-ha! "Speedy recovery, Bernadette. I miss you. And I hope Flaherty gets pneumonia."

James frowned. "Why do you think he said that?"

"I'll remind you two," Moira said. "If you don't know, James, Ollie always had his eyes on my baby sister. You beat him."

"I never realized that," Bernadette said. "As long as I've known him, I never…"

"I think it's time for you two to take a walk. Get some fresh air."

They wrapped themselves with heavy sweaters, woolen caps, and scarves around their necks and ventured out for a walk. They walked along the pipe railing all the way down to the Haven Hotel. Cool breezes from the harbor greeted them, and the kittiwakes called from their cliffside roosts. "They'll be leaving soon," Bernadette said.

"I hate to see them go."

They turned around and made their way back uphill, all the way to the Centra Store. They rested on a bench there, then walked back to the inn. "Moira was right, James, so fresh out there, how do you feel?"

"Much better." Back in the sickroom, she said, "Know what? I think we should have a short ride to our song! Wouldn't that be grand?"

"A quickie? Grand, indeed."

She winked and put their song on. "Not long. Let's do it. No facey." She put her hands and knees on the bed, inviting him. He mounted from behind, against her smooth buttocks, and thrust until she grunted in pleasure. "All over," she sighed, "A true quickie!"

Both resting on the bed, James said, "Let's plan for buying our rings."

Eyes closed, she whispered, "A good idea. Why don't we take big sister with us to pick out our rings? I know just the place: Glencara's in Wexford. That's where Tony and I picked Moira's."

"We can take her to lunch. She's one groovy chick."

"I know just the place. La Cote. A wee bit Frenchy, but I think she'll like it. Maybe we can get Mom and Dad to keep her little ones."

"Let's do it." And they rested away the afternoon.

Moira and Caitlin loved the messages, and big sister liked to have a goo, which is lovely Irish slang for shopping and bargaining. The couple wanted claddagh birthstone rings, so Moira carefully examined the choices at Glencara's. James' stone was topaz; Bernadette's ruby. Moira found the settings with real stones, and they were expensive, but James said he didn't care. He wanted the best.

After the shopping, they surprised Moira by taking her to La Cote on Wexford's waterfront. They each selected different kinds of fish. Bernadette ordered Sancerre, a white wine from the Loire Valley. When the waiter brought it, James pointed to his fiancée for tasting. She went through the usual routine and declared it "Perfect! Citrus, light fruit, and some earth tones."

She and James toasted Moira, who said, "It's a good thing you've left the sick room, Bernadette, because I need some help in the bar tonight."

"I know," Bernadette said. "First, let's help James settle in his new home."

"Then I'll be visiting with the civil marriage forms. I didn't realize how complete it would be. I already filled in my little sister's part. But, James, you'll have to answer some questions. We'll take care of all that this afternoon, agreed?"

They drove back to Dunmore East and thoroughly cleaned the sick room, then all three returned to James' bungalow. "So, James, what is your national origin?"

"American, of course."

"The government wants specifics."

"Oh, my grandmother's family immigrated from Germany, and she married my Irish grandfather. My mother's family came from West Virginia."

"They want names."

"Catherine Elizabeth and Dorsey Dell, John Thompson and Florence."

"Good," Moira answered. Bernadette sat on the end of the bed and listened intently. "They want to know your financial situation, James."

He thought, then he told her, "About $1.2 million gross worth and $10,700 a month net worth."

"O Mo Dia!" The sisters exclaimed together. "You're rich!" Moira said.

"Not rich, but well off. Part of that monthly will last fifteen years, but I figure the investment funds will more than make up for that during the time. I already told your father about this."

"I think the government will be impressed. I can fill in the rest. Thank you, James."

"Thank YOU, big sister. I appreciate it."

"Get some rest, Bernadette. You'll be working tonight."

"Aye."

"I'm going with her," James declared. "During break we can sit in the lounge."

They settled on the bed. "James. I got a chance to review your memoir in the sick room."

"How far are you now?"

"Where Rickie-Bear got killed. So tragic. I don't know how you and Ardal survived all that violence."

"I did. Ardal didn't."

"You must really miss him."

"He was my brother. The worst part was I lost contact with him. After just one letter."

"Ironic. An American, an Irishman brought together by the violence of war. La guerra es horrible."

"Yeah," he began to nod off. They napped together.

* * *

The bar had a thin crowd, and Bernadette spent most of the time sitting on her favorite stool. James sat at the end closest to her. Ollie Savage arrived and sat at the opposite end of the bar. For the first time in days, James was enjoying a whiskey with a pint. He sipped slowly. Ollie ordered a Bulmers and barely touched it. He fixed his eyes on Bernadette, then turned to James. "Hey, Jimmy. Are ya?"

"Hey Ollie. Pneumonia. Really?"

"No worries. A joke. Do you hunt?"

"Never did. Why?"

"I have a friend I hunt with down in Killarney Lakes. We have our guns locked at the club."

"Ollie," Bernadette said. "I didn't know you hunted."

"Oh yeah. Small game, deer. Whatever I can get with my .22 swift. Did you ever handle a gun, Jimmy?"

James remained silent. Bernadette's cheek dimpled a smile. "Here and there," he answered, "but I have no more use for them."

"Pity. I could teach you. I'm a pretty good shot, if I say so."

Bernadette's dimples expanded up her cheek.

"Get me another, Bernadette."

"You haven't touched the one I poured for you, Ollie."

"I don't have to explain myself. Just do what you're told, please. By the way, I congratulate you and Mr. Flaherty." He held his glass high for a toast. "May you have many children and a happy life together."

James returned. "Thanks, Ollie."

Delany arrived. "Why don't you break, honey? I'll cover."

Bernadette and James moved around the bar to their favorite place in the den. The peat fire burned with a low, glowing light. James brought an orange mineral for her.

"This is so boring," she said. "I can't wait until eleven."

James thought a few minutes and said to her, "Do you know what a narcissist is?"

"A little, why?"

"I think Ollie is. He seems to think he rules everybody in the world. He's obviously insecure, but he tries to hide it. He has no feelings for anyone but himself, and he's insanely jealous."

"I don't see that. Ollie and I grew up together. He's always been nice to me."

"I think Ollie could be quite dangerous, maybe violent. He's made me his enemy, so I'm the one who would be his target."

"He is a bit carlow, but we're engaged. Why would he bother us?"

"That's the way they are. Believe me, I've seen a few in my life."

"Let's quit talking about him. I came up with a good idea. Why don't we go golfing? I already know how you play."

"Good idea. Let's make it soon. We haven't played since South Carolina."

the hump

Long Binh had changed. It was like stepping into a mini-America. We saw two hospitals, an Olympic-size swimming pool, a multiplex movie theater, two restaurants Chinese(Chinese and steakhouse9) and a brand new mess hall. Relaxing now, we had turned in our weapons to the armorer for repair and exchanged our rotten uniforms for new ones. Then we passed headquarters. It now had a garden of green grass, flowers and banana trees. We saw LBJ (Long Binh Jail) and the PX. A new USO and three batteries of 155-millimeter cannons. Sand-bagged walls surrounded the hootches. The domestic labor force did the REMF's laundry; the clothes hung out to dry. Most remarkably, a very large EM Club covered a long patch of ground. But they still burned shit; the clouds of foul diesel fires lifted above the camp in black plumes.

"These REMF's have it made," McKenzie said. "Look at all this."

"I'd like to eat a real breakfast up in that mess hall," Ardal added.

We sat on the porch of the wooden barracks fashioned for troops on stand down. Lee bought a bottle of Jack Daniels from the Class VI store. We shared it with the free beer afforded us. I said to Ardal, "We can go into town and get laid."

"Sounds great. It's been so long I carry a picture of my hand in my shirt pocket."

"Haven't you heard?" McKenzie said. "The General put Bien Hoa off limits."

"All those beautiful women. All those seedy bars."

Ardal said, "We need a new stash of consa."

"I guess we'll have to wait 'til we get back to the 'ville," I said.

Lee said, "We're goin' to have a great three days here. I'm anxious to go to that newfangled EM Club."

"Me, too," I added. "Do any of you guys feel homesick?"

"Not really," Ardal said. "This is all make believe. I think I'm in a mirage."

"Well put," McKenzie said.

The battalion offered free grilled steaks for us. We could smell lobster and crab boiling. The rainy season had almost ended, but we still had a twenty minute shower in late afternoon, after which steam rose from the ground, which did not alleviate much the smell of burning shit. We sipped liquor and took long swallows of the cold beer.

"I guess we're hardcore stomachs now," said McKenzie. "I'm gonna look around for some consa."

"That would be better than this shit," I said. "Gettin' high in this wonderland would be quite a trip."

While we were drinking, Lieutenant Sam and Doc Joyner approached. "Settled in?" Sam asked.

"Hey Lieutenant. What do you think of this wonderland?"

"Too brief for us, I'm afraid. Just got word we're going on a jungle hump."

"What brought this on?" I asked.

"Intelligence wants us to support the 173rd Airborne. Ninth Vietcong Division is operating in an area northeast."

"173rd. What the fuck, over!"

"At least it's dry land."

"Yeah," I said. "But the jungle won't be dry. Too much humidity."

"Have fun. Rest. Early morning one day from now."

* * *

After drinking our fill, we decided to eat a steak. McKenzie returned. "Any luck?"

"I scored four J's from a clerk at Brigade. He told me that there are some hootch girls sellin' pussy."

"Do we need to pitch in for the dope?"

"He gave 'em to us. Since we're here for stand-down."

"We're on our way to get a steak. Wear this booze off. Join us."

The line at the Battalion mess tent thinned enough we didn't have to wait long. We got ribeye to order and lobster tails to go with them. The cook asked us if we wanted crab legs, and we piled those on, too. We took the food to benches set up for us, with coolers of beer nearby. We ate voraciously and drank down beer.

Ardal asked, "Whaddya want to do now?"

"Rest. Let's go back to our barracks and set up our cots."

Sitting on the wooden steps again, we had to decide what to do.

Ardal said, "I hope they make eggs to order at that mess hall."

"Bacon and sausages," I added, "and potatoes, grits, and toast."

Lee said, "It sounds so good. I like the wheetena."

"Everything," I added.

"I couldn't live another day," Ardal said, "with C-rations in it."

"Well," McKenzie piped, "If you get peaches and a decent entree, you can toss the rest of it."

Lee and McKenzie went into the barracks.

"Why don't we go exploring a bit? I'd like to see the USO."

We reached the building. "Welcome," an American lady greeted us, then showed us around: pool tables and ping pong, and music booths where we could listen to country, pop, rock, and even classical. We viewed the small library of books and magazines and tried out the cushioned sofa there. "Thanks, ma'am, we can take it from here.'

Ardal beamed. "Let's go to the EM Club."

"Yeah, maybe a couple more beers."

Only two soldiers and the sergeant first class occupied the place. Ardal and I took a table. The two soldiers approached us. One of them asked, "Are you combat soldiers?"

"Yes," I answered. "On stand-down."

"Wow. I admire you guys. Who you with?"

"Old Guard."

"I heard you were Rangers."

"You heard right." Ardal shot me a sharp look.

Why not, I thought, *we operate like Rangers.*

The other soldier, a PFC, said, "Let me buy you guys a beer. What's your brand?"

"Anything will be okay, thanks."

The one asked so many rapid-fire questions we couldn't answer. The other just sat dumbly, without so much as a word or two.

"Listen," Ardal finally said. "I appreciate all your compliments, but we're tired. Do you mind if we sit alone and enjoy our beers? No offense."

"Oh, yeah. Listen. It's good to meet you. It's a true honor to know you."

We silently drank our beers and left. "I can't stand it," I said. "They have it so nice here and can't leave us alone."

"I wanted to punch them out," Ardal said. "Just one would do it."

"Hold your temper, Shea. We're just passin' through."

"Let's go back and get high," Ardal said.

"Roger on that."

We gathered with Lee and McKenzie. "This dope's powerful," McKenzie said after a couple of hits. "The clerk said it's Cambodian Red. I never heard of it."

Shea added, "I'm really trippin.'"

"So am I."

We fixated on the night horizon. "What are those purple lights dancing over there?" Lee said.

"I don't know, but it's sure pretty."

"Look at that bright light shining. It's moving fast."

"Wow! Fast. Look! It's climbing!"

"A freedom bird!"

"Whoa! I can't wait for mine. Back in the world!"

"The world. Back to normal. Away from this shit. Just think of it; we'll be free forever. Back in the world."

"Yeah. We're still stuck here in Vietnam, Republic of."

"I hate this place. We're gettin' wasted, and people back in the world livin' normal lives."

"Fuckin' round-eyes. Eatin' good food."

Ardal said, "I smell bacon sizzling on the grill."

"I can smell sausage," I returned.

"What's that?" Lee said. "The sweet aroma of oatmeal. I'll put brown sugar on it."

"I like toast. Real toast; not those stale crackers in our 'C's"

"Oh-h-h. I can't wait 'til morning. I'm so hungry."

"And then, we're going to the jungle."

"I've never been on a jungle hump," Ardal said. "What's it like?"

"Brutal." I answered. "Hot, steamy, hostile. But at least on dry land."

McKenzie added, "We'll have to carry those heavy rucksacks. Makes the hump more miserable."

"For some reason," I said. "I just can't get that Stevie Wonder song out of my head. It always pops up on a jungle hump."

"What song?"

"Like an old dusty road, I get weary from the load."

"Movin' on. Movin' on."

"A place in the sun!"

"That's it. 'Like this tired, troubled earth, I been roamin' since my birth."

"Movin' on. Movin' on."

"Great song."

Lee said, "Very apropos."

"I still smell breakfast," Ardal said. "It's so wonderful."

"Why don't we get some sleep?" McKenzie said.

"Hey, Sarge, what about those hootch girls.? Did you find out?"

"Apparently, they're kept a secret. I guess these REMFs want to keep them for themselves."

"That's okay," Lee said. "I don't fancy payin' for it anyway."

Ardal and I glanced and smiled. We were thinking about Co Hue back in the 'ville.

We marched to the mess hall first thing in the early morning and saw others from our company. We dapped and repeated, "What the fuck? Over."

We were impressed with the new mess hall and formed a long line. When Ardal and I were about to order, two soldiers with worn uniforms jumped in front.

"Hey man," Ardal said. "We're next."

"Sorry," one of the soldiers said. "We have to hurry."

"Why?"

"Casualty escort. Seven in all: three KIA, four WIA."

I asked, "Are they gonna make it?"

"Probably not."

"Who're you guys with?" Lee asked.

"One Seventy-Third Airborne. We have to hurry back. Thought we'd grab a nice breakfast before."

"By all means," McKenzie said. "We'll be joining you in a couple days."

"You don't look like field soldiers with those brand new fatigues. We thought you were new guys."

"Not hardly," Ardal said. "We're with the 199th."

"Oh. The Rangers."

"Yeah, and we're op-conning you."

"Get ready. Pretty nasty up there. Thanks for letting us through."

"You bet. Enjoy. Might be your last meal."

After chow, we gathered at the barracks. "Two J's left."

"I thought you got four," Ardal said.

"I mean after this one. We'll get high two more times before we go on the hump."

While passing the J, Ardal said, "What a wonderful breakfast. How 'bout those two guys from the 173rd?"

Lee said, "Makin' me nervous about the hump."

"Look! That shimmer over there. Looks like rising waves."

Lounging in the shade near the barracks, we watched the traffic buzz past us, especially the Lambros sounding like stinging insects.

As brilliantly white clouds held steady in the morning calm; we felt the same stillness, and tried to reach up and touch them. An old man walked along the highway, sporting long, white hair and Ho Chi Minh whiskers falling below his chest. He wore white Ao Babas (those pajamas the peasants like to wear).

"Damn!" Ardal exhaled. "I think I see the Christ." He crossed himself.

Doc Joyner and Lieutenant Sam came back early for inspection. We tried to straighten up.

"You guys be careful with that stuff," Sam said. "I don't want to have to bail you out of jail before the hump."

And we exploded. "SNARK! SNARK! The hump… we go on the hump… SNORK!"

Sam shook his head and left. Thomas followed.

"Did… SNARK! You… HUH!… See that… HA!"

"Yeah. The hump. the hump… maybe we can find those hootch girls and… SNARK!… And… WHOOP!… hump… them!"

"You're crazy. The… ONLY! BOOOM! Hump… GAWK! THE HUMP… We'll… BE… FUCKIN' the jungle."

"Okay… Okay… Settle down." It was Mckenzie, trying to collect us, which only made us laugh and giggle even more.

Lee took a deep breath. "Calm down, now. We have to eat lunch soon and drink more whiskey."

"WHISKEY! SNARK! Did you…SNORT! Say whiskey? WHISKEY! YEAH! Drink…HA! More… SCREECH! WHISKEY! Man…WHISKEY! WHAT THE FUCK, OVER!"

Soon enough, our high mellowed.

Lee said, "I can't believe it. Hallucination. HAIL CAMBODIA!"

"HAIL CAMBODIA! HAIL CAMBODIA!"

"Let's savor. I see steak and lobster in our future."

"And more…SNORK! WHISKEY! HUH-H-H-H!"

"Maybe another J, too."

We ate our steaks hungrily; Ardal liked rare, and the rest of us preferred medium. We each got a lobster tail; Ardal took two. Then he begged them for more. He finally talked the cook to boil himself a whole one.

"How are you going to deal with that, Shea?" McKenzie said.

"That's what entrenching tools are for."

We went to the armory and drew our weapons. Bright and shiny. All we needed now was a thin coat of oil. We were given new bandoliers that could hold eight magazines each. We had been trained to put the empty back in the bandolier so the enemy couldn't get their hands on them.

"Let's go back and hallucinate some more!" McKenzie said.

"Hey," Ardal said. "We still have one left."

McKenzie returned. "Better save it for the 'ville."

"I can't wait to get back to the 'ville," I said.

* * *

Next morning, the company filed past the north gate of Long Binh. We had to march a single column. Ardal and I, armed with machetes, went point. Two flanks. Two rear, two slacks. About a quarter mile, we penetrated. The triple canopy created a steam bath effect; sweat poured. Our vision blurred as we sweated over our lashes. We had to keep wiping. Ardal and I started hacking brushes. We whacked above our heads, then swiped down and across below our knees to make a path. Exhausted, we passed the machetes to the slack and took their place. When they were beat, we switched back to give them some rest. Once, we came upon a massive spider web, with the huge creature poised to strike prey. We decided to hack around it. Green snakes hung from vines with foliage of different shades. Occasional light streams provided drama. The heat became worse. While outside the forest, temperatures stayed in the upper 80s. The jungle steam would easily be in the 100s. We came to a narrow stream in a bamboo plantation. One by one, we carefully filled our canteens with cool, fresh water. Leeches started to appear, and McKenzie found one engorged from his wrist to elbow. We burned them off with lighted cigarettes. Past the stream we continued hacking. Suddenly Lorenzo slapped and wriggled; red ants, nesting in trees in large moving balls, were falling all over him. Frantic, he stripped off his clothes. We helped him brush off the voracious insects as some dug their heads into his skin and delivered painful stings, leaving him crying and cursing.

We saw an orangutan lazily turning his head to us.

"That thing's huge," Ardal said. The beast suddenly leapt on the trail and threatened by beating its chest and waving his powerful fists.. We saw the rest of the colony scatter into the forest. We kept slowly moving until BOOM and screaming! We crouched, thinking it would be a mortar, but we didn't hear the sizzling of incoming. We carefully looked up and saw in horror: a vine had caught Lee's grenade pin. He lay on the ground now in shock. We saw that his lower body was nearly cut in two. His bowels opened to the putrid air; nothing left of his genitalia.

"Shoot me! Shoot me! My life is over. Please shoot me!"

He died before our eyes. A dust-off was called in. We waited for thirty minutes, ourselves feeling gutted, until the medivac could pick up the body. The bird had to drop a penetrator basket to retrieve Lee. "Goddamn you, Lee!" Ardal and I screamed in tears.

McKenzie was frozen, but Turner ordered us to continue the hump.

Hacking and hacking, we hoped to come across a new crop of bamboo. On and on. No time for crying. Through a tunnel of steam. We saw tiny brown two-step snakes camouflaged on brown twigs. We called them two-step snakes, for once you got bitten, you took two steps and collapsed. Fortunately, not enough venom to kill, but enough to make us sick with dry heaves and dizziness. Finally, after a quarter mile, we broke through to clear terrain. We saw a hill rising above a field of elephant grass. Turner took the horn. "Big six, this is six, over."

"Six, this is big six, oscar, over."

"This is six. Objective reached. Waiting for instructions, over."

"Uh, this is big six. Dig in and hold perimeter, over."

"This is six. Roger-wilco, out."

"Okay. You heard the man. Start digging."

We unfolded our entrenching tools and started chinking the hard dirt. "Not as good as cracking lobster, eh," I said to Ardal.

"Lobster, is it?"

We chopped and dug at the ground, throwing clods to the side. It was a hard, long process. I removed a large chunk of dirt and uncovered a nest of insects. I tried to pick one up with my shovel and felt a quick sting.

"Ow!" Looking closer, I realized what those insects were. SCORPIONS! "Get back, everybody. Scorpions." My wrist started to burn. I could feel the heat crawling up to my elbow.

Doc Joyner came and treated and bandaged the sting. "You'll be ok; they're too small to do any real damage."

"It still hurts like hell."

Sam came with a can of repellent spray. He pushed the nozzle and lit the spray with a lighter. That was the tecāique we used on the balls of red ants. It worked. He killed most of the scorpions, and the others quickly crawled away.

"Go back digging your foxholes."

Once we settled into the two-man foxholes, Ardal volunteered for the first two-hour shift. I tried to sleep, but exhaustion prevented even a quick doze. So I sat watching Shea peering intently over the top as the sky had fallen into a soft darkness…darkness…cold, terrifying darkness.

"FUCK YOU! FUCK YOU! RE-UP, RE-UP! FUCK YOU!"

Ardal nudged me. "What was that?" he whispered.

"That's just a gecko; tokay. We call them the fuck you lizards."

"What was that other noise?"

"Re-up bird. They're nocturnal. Need to scrounge around jungle floor for food. Harmless."

"Loud. I thought it was VC laughing at us."

"It's ok; take it easy and watch."

In the middle of the night, while I was on watch, I sensed tiny movements through the trees. Dark shadows were coming toward us. I awoke Ardal. "Shea. Ardal. Get up. I see people coming."

"I see them, too," Ardal answered. He aimed his rifle.

I covered the barrel. "Don't shoot. They're just probin' us. Checkin' our perimeter if there are any weak spots. Wait 'em out."

Somebody tossed a concussion grenade. The shock hurt our ears. The shadows moved away and disappeared. Turner crawled to Sam's position and whispered, "We need to send out ambushes. One squad per platoon."

"Out there? In the dark? Through that elephant grass?"

"Send your squad to that gully down there. Night march."

Our squad was selected. With Lee gone, McKenzie had to carry his M60. We all carried belts of ammo. We moved slowly. The elephant grass was razor sharp and easily cut our arms and faces. We had to feel our way through it. In an hour, we reached the gully and set up a linear. The machine gun position was far left flank. Grenade launchers right flank. Rifles in between. We now knew the VC were everywhere around us. We didn't know, but battalion orders were to make contact with the 9th VC division. My wrist burned up to my elbow.

Captain Turner's assessment was correct. He knew the Viet Cong liked to probe positions in the early evening. They chose to attack just before daylight. That way, they could overrun, kill the enemy before daylight, and then flee from any air support or artillery. We were too far away for 155s support. Attack helicopters and jet strafing would be the only support we could muster.

We waited for three or four hours before we saw movement coming through the gulch. They must've been confident now, on a flanking movement to attack the hill. We watched their careful movement until more came into our kill zone. Now, up to ninety or so, they stopped. More Charlies joined. Now, more than a hundred, our machine gun was put in a position to fire straight into the enemy line. We patiently waited, savoring our good luck. My wrist now was flaming. I wanted to complain, but I didn't dare compromise our advantaged position. McKenzie held the machine gun at the ready. He couldn't call in artillery, and gunships would be too risky; it was all on our shoulders. We didn't know if any other squads positioned nearby saw. Us, and us alone. Outnumbered by a large margin, but with the advantage of surprise. And they were bunched up. My wrist was on fire now. When no more enemies appeared, McKenzie let loose with the 60. Tracers streaked into their ranks. Grenade explosions thumped on them, and our rifle fire followed. They fired back desperately. They were using SKS rifles with green tracers. Our murderous fire overwhelmed them, dropping many down. The Charlies scattered, carrying their wounded and dragging their dead comrades.

"One-three, one-three, this is six, over."

"This is one-three, over."

"What's your sit-rep, over."

"This is one-three. Made contact with superior force, over."

"Any casualties, over?"

"Not a scratch. Many enemy casualties, over."

"One-three. Hold position, over."

"Roger, Wilco, over."

The morning light finally appeared. We saw no enemy casualties, and we dropped our guard. My arm became worse, as the fire reached up to my shoulder. I couldn't straighten my elbow. I could still carry my weapon on my left shoulder, but the pain in my right wrist was dizzying. I shivered. I sweated. Chills and heat at the same time.

"Six, this is one-three. We need to return to the perimeter. One man sick."

"One-three; this is six. How bad?"

"Very,"

"Okay, return immediately."

We made our way through the elephant grass and back to the perimeter.

Joyner removed my bandage for inspection. He immediately gave me morphine, "You're gonna have to be dusted off."

It took the chopper at least thirty minutes to reach us. I was escorted in; medic inside took over. He checked my vitals as the morphine had taken effect; I was so drowsy, I had to fight off sleep. I saw the canopied tropical forest pass below. The pilot flew at maximum speed, making the trees skim by and quickly turn into a map-like feature. We must've humped twenty miles but flew past in what seemed like ten minutes. The bird landed at the Field Hospital in Long Binh, where I was rushed to the emergency room and prepared for surgery. The nurse turned me on the left side, as later I learned the doctor didn't want me to see the procedure. The morphine put me into a near sleep state. I could feel the ice numbing on my wrist, and then only the pull of the scalpel. Then I drifted asleep.

I awoke in a ward, on a soft bed with two pillows and a pain-free arm except for the soreness. I fell back to sleep.

Later in the afternoon, Joyner, Sam, Ardal, and McKenzie came for a visit. "You had a close call," Sam said.

Joyner added, "Very close. The doctor told me you fought the poison, but infection set in. He pulled long streams of puss out of you. He said if the infection reached your heart, you'd be dead."

"I'm glad you made it," McKenzie said. "We can trip again."

"Trip again," Ardal said. "I'm so happy you survived this trip."

I asked, "Are you guys goin' back to the 'ville?"

"They're keeping us here," Sam said. "Another mission down to Bearcat, then up the Nui Vai."

"Get well, James, so you can join us."

"Yuh," I answered. "I miss the 'ville."

Ardal flashed that familiar smile; he was thinking about Co Hue. I was, too.

irish handshake

Bernadette didn't bother to knock on the front door. She just came in.

"You look like you're dressed for golf."

"A family outing with daddy, brother-in-law Tony, and my dear friends."

"Harper and Caroline play?"

"Indeed."

"Ellsbeth?"

"No. She never took up the game."

"That makes me happy. I need some relaxing."

"So, James. Straight stableford. If I win, you'll have to work a week for me at the inn."

"Where will you be, then?"

"Dublin, of course."

"Maybe an old boyfriend?"

"You're my fella, James!"

"Hmmm. Okay. If I win, I think you should clean my place 'til it's sparkle city."

She wrinkled a smile. "You're on."

"Do we need to shake hands?"

"James! You don't trust your fiancée?" She pointed to his bed.

"Getting dressed, straightaway!"

***

Faithlegg presented a cloudy day without the threat of rain. The girls dressed alike: navy blue slacks, white blouses, plaid vests, and powder blue hats. James wondered if they knew powder blue was an infantry color. They looked quite attractive.

Jack wore a blue turtle neck under a green shell sweater. James wore a white mock with a light, red shell. Tony's, a golf shirt covered by an orange sweater vest. The women hit off the ladies' tee, while the men waited on their tees. They hit into the green with short irons, hidden by the woods. Bernadette approached the second tee holding her ball over her head. "Birdie!" James shrank a bit.

"Do you two have a bet?" asked Jack.

"Kinda."

"What was—oh never mind. I can only imagine. Don't you know how good a golfer Bernadette is?"

"Yes. We played a round in South Carolina. She beat me by four strokes."

"James. You're in for it," Tony said. "You better be on the top of your game."

"I'm not worried, Tony. I can beat her."

"Should we start?"

"Wait 'til they hit off the second tee," Tony answered.

With honors, Bernadette pulled her driver into the decayed gorse left of the narrow, uphill fairway. "Ah hah!" James barked.

She had to drop out and use a wood for her third shot. She struck a high draw close to the green. James said, "I know that beautiful swing of hers."

She hit wedge onto the putting surface. The girls exalted, "Birdie!"

James gulped. 'Damn, she holed out!' "Okay," said Tony. "Your honors, James."

They each hit long irons and easily reached the green with wedges. James parred; Jack and Tony bogeyed. The second hole was bogeyed by all three. The third parred. When they reached the downhill par-four number four, James could see the girls' hats. They weren't yelling or screaming, so he thought, *That's it. She got off to a fast start, but was slowing down. Hope is still there.* Many a time he'd got off to a fast start then sputtered. He knew she made seven points on the first three holes; he had made five so far.

They played down, then around and back up hill to the ninth. Pars and bogeys, no birdies, and two doubles. Maybe the scores would even out over the first nine. The golf course held flower boxes here and there with shrubs. Maybe a symbol for what lay ahead? But it could be the same symbol for her. The back nine had consecutive par fives; one long, one short. As they approached the River Suir, wind picked up to strong gusts. They played to a green close to the river; adjusted to low shots and extra club to reach it. Standing on the green, Tony said. "This river brought in two invasions. First Norwegians, then Longshanks."

"The Vikings were looking for farmland, and Cromwell was looking for Catholics," James opined.

"The Vikings were just as vicious," Tony replied. "But means led to different ends."

"So which do you hate the most?"

"Longshanks, for sure. A true devil, ironically, fighting for religion—his only."

They turned with the wind behind them, adding ten or fifteen yards to their shots. They clubbed up and hit more lofted fairway woods. When they turned to the eighteenth, a long uphill par four, the men scored only one bogey. "This hole always does me in," Jack complained. "Doubles every time."

They walked to the clubhouse. The girls stood waiting and smiling. "How did you fellas get around?" Harper asked. "We scored forty-nine."

Father added up. "We got forty-nine , too. Huh."

Inside, they sat at a round table and shared pints. The girls held roses behind their backs: Harper and Caroline each presented a white rose to James; Bernadette a red rose.

"My love is a red, red rose," she said proudly and winked, and each girl kissed his cheek.

"Hey, look," Harper said. "Their sweaters are the colors of our flag. Did you gents plan that?"

"Coincidence," said Tony.

"So, James," Bernadette said, "our combined points came out even, but I made twenty-three and you twenty-one. I win."

She raised her glass again and winked again. Jack added the scorecard again, "I made a mistake. James, you made twenty-three, too."

"What'll we do? Playoff, or draw straws."

"That's between you two."

Bernadette said, "Fingers." They shook three times, threw out a match from James, and a paper from Bernadette.

"Match burns paper," James said. "Get the bucket and mop! I'll see you in the morning."

"Goodbye, Dublin. I shall miss you." They all ordered the lunch special offered.

"Okay everybody. James' favorite: lamb kidneys."

Harper said, "My favorite, too."

James said, "I haven't seen Ollie Savage lately. Did he leave?"

"Went to Wexford to visit a friend," Jack offered.

"Damn. I was hopin' he'd be here to see my triumph."

"You don't always get what you wish."

"He's carlow. He gives me the creeps," Harper said.

James added, "He's sick."

"Oh-h," Bernadette said. "He's a jagoff, but harmless."

Everybody looked at her. Caroline asked, "What's a jag-off?"

"Something I learned in Pittsburgh."

"What's it mean?"

"A very annoying person, but harmless."

"I wouldn't say that," James countered. "The little I know about psychology, I still say he's narcissistic."

"Narcissistic, is it?"

"Extreme, in my opinion."

"Extreme, is it.?"

"People like him don't see the world the way we do. They have their own reality. That's what makes them so egoistic. His fixation on you makes me think he could be dangerous. I've experienced men like that in the Army."

The group finished lunch together, and the golfers all said their goodbyes. Back at the inn, "I'm tired," Bernadette said. "I think I need a nap."

"A nap would be so nice."

"Then, let's go home."

"Straightaway?"

"Indeed."

As they lay spooning, she said, "If we'd been married when you were in Vietnam, I'd worry so much."

"You don't have to worry now. It's over."

"Is it really? Don't you think about it?"

"Every day now. It's coming back."

"Can I make it better?"

"You already have. Being with you makes me so happy."

She turned and kissed him. "What's with you lads smoking marijuana? Addicts is what ye were."

"It was harmless, girl. Gave us needed escape." He yawned and dozed off. He saw Lee and Ardal. "Get down, get down! Don't you see? They're comin' after us! They're gonna kill us. Get down!"

He awoke, heart pounding. *She just had to bring it up.* He rolled away from her, tucked his hands under his head, and went back to sleep in the fetal position.

When they awoke, she announced she had to work that evening. "May I come back for the night?"

"This is your home." James answered. "In fact, I'll go with you; maybe go on the tear."

"Don't overdo it, dear. I still have use."

They dressed and went to the inn. She took her corner seat with James near her. Tourist season had ended, and a few hearty souls had checked in amid the colder weather.

"Pint?" asked Bernadette.

"And a whisky, too."

"James, are you really going on the tear?"

"I'm going to have a grand evening; my own craic."

"Craic, is it? Who're you going to joke with, me?"

"If I have to. The new guests may come for some food and drink. Maybe I can strike up a party. Then we can throw down."

She stared blankly, then whispered, "Throw down?"

James ordered a large basket of chips.

"You want malt?" Bernadette asked.

"I'm American. We don't like malt on our French fries."

They settled in. New guests did come down to the bar; Ireland makes the best Guinness. I'm from Wales, but the Guinness here is so much better. Must be the water."

"River Liffey," Bernadette said.

As more guests appeared, friendly conversation continued, until the man said, "I don't like Americans." So James moved to a table to enjoy his drink alone. *I don't like Americans, indeed. Fuck off* Eleven o'clock Bernadette shut down and turned off the lights. She locked up and dragged the fluthered James back to the bungalow. She gently laid him on the big bed and kissed him. She lay beside him and quickly fell asleep.

Next morning, she changed back into her golf outfit, without the hat. She stood over James. "I guess I should go and get the cleaning stuff."

He opened gritty eyes and yawned. "You really mean it. I thought it was just a joke." His head hurt, and his back was stiff.

"I believe in paying off bets."

"I do, too, but this isn't necessary."

"Pick up your things before I get back."

She left, and thirty minutes later, she came back with a steel bucket, brushes, and a mop.

"Why don't you get down on your hands and knees?" He joked. "I like to feel like the man of the house. That's where you should be."

She lifted her head and scowled without a word.

He crossed over to the bathroom. "Yeah. When we get married, I think you should dye your hair black and put on eye makeup that makes you look Asian. I'm hittin' the jacks, and I expect you…"

WHACK! Her hard slap knocked him down by the sink. Blood oozed. Another whack pushed him to the wall. "Feckin Gobshite!" she yelled and slammed the door.

He crawled to the bed, feeling the sting, and sat. *Why do I say things in jest that get me into trouble? She took it too seriously. She'll come around realizing I didn't mean what I said…her temper will quickly pass, and I will be forgiven. I surely hope so.*

He couldn't go out; he was too embarrassed to be seen like this. The purple had spread from his cheek to his ear alongside the drying scab. Miserable in his isolation, he wondered if she was really through with him. He replayed their last words more than once. *Fucking idiot. How do you do it? No wonder.* Four days later, the color had faded, but he still wasn't ready to show his face to the town. He was finishing his sad morning tea when there was a knock on the door. He was relieved to see Bernadette smiling.

"I'm so sorry I'm an idiot! Can you please forgive me?" and drew her inside, his hands shaking.

"James, I have something to tell you."

"You didn't finish me off."

"I missed."

"I'll say."

"I missed! Don't you understand, I missed! I'm up the pole."

"Was it cold? Wait a minute. We only did a quickie in the sick room. How—They looked into each other's eyes and said, "PITTSBURGH! "What an irony. I was conceived and born there.' "How do you know for sure?" Wrapping her in his arms.

"I already have cravings. For pizza, I can't get enough."

"Pizza? Where do you get it around here?"

"Moira's made it for me."

"I can go to Waterford and buy many boxes. We can freeze it, like I did when I bought dozens of boxes in Pittsburgh. I'd take it to South Carolina and freeze it. I bought calzones, too. Freeze it. Do they make calzones in town? Or maybe some stromboli's. They're just as good. I used to eat calzones all the time. I like the ones with capicola and pepperoni, with mozzarella, bell peppers, and onion. You think you'd like that? I think so. Moira and I can make good tomato sauce for you. I can buy pepperoni and capicola at Centra. They have to carry it.

If not, I'll go all the way to Dublin. Just think of it. All you need for your cravings. To make a strong baby. We'd be blessed. Maybe black hair like an Italian. Remember that guy at the hotel bar? I'll bet he loved pizza. And pasta too. Do you like pasta? We can make it in different ways. You'll love it. First there's—

"Houl yer whisht!"

"You don't have to yell."

"You're rambling like an eejit. Just stop, please."

He caressed her back. "I guess I'm excited!"

"I know! Hopefully, you'll calm down."

He sat her on the bed and touched her belly. "Feel it movin' around?"

"Too early. Oh, James, I'm so happy."

"I love you, Bernadette. I'm so proud. I'm a man! I'm a man! Look at me!"

"Eejit again."

"Did you tell your parents yet?"

"I'm afraid to. Only my sister knows."

"We should see them together."

"But we're not married yet. I don't know how they'll react."

"I think we'll make them happy. After all, we'll be married soon."

She crossed herself, "Let's go, then."

They were lucky in catching Delany and Jack together. "Mr. and Mrs. Bohan! We have some news." He cleared his throat.

Bernadette blurted, "I'm up the pole."

Delany and Jack, unphased, looked at the couple with warm eyes and smiled broadly. "A new grandchild!" Jack said. Delany hugged James and her daughter. "I'm so happy for you!"

"I hope it's a girl," her father said.

James said, "I hope it's a boy."

"Do you know the due date?" her mother asked.

"We just found out; maybe July or August."

"Jack! This is so exciting!" Turning to Bernadette, she said, "Did you tell anybody else?"

She didn't want to hurt their feelings. She'd shared with Moira and her dear friends. "No."

Jack said, "We should spread the news. Happy times."

An hour later James looked at the requested pizza as it was presented by Moira. "Ham, bacon, blood sausage, and some pork. You must be craving meat!"

James got a pint of the black stuff; she got a Bulmers." She ate a large slice, at least a quarter of the pie.

"This is good." He was impressed by Moira's additional toppings. "I won't have to go to Waterford after all."

She rested on the bed while James sat at the small table and scribbled corrections on his manuscript. He joined her and napped until she stirred. "It's Wednesday. Disco tonight."

"You feel up to it? It's going to be cold tonight."

"I feel fine." She held him tightly. She kissed him hard and twirled. She slipped her hand inside his trousers and caressed him longer. "You want to ride now?"

"Last thing on my mind."

"It'll feel good," she teased.

She unzipped him and gave him a hand job.

* * *

Light flurries softly in the night air. She shivered and reached for his hand, as they hurried along the sidewalk. "Freezing out, are you ok?"

"I'm fine," she answered.

Inside Slaney's, they were surprised to see a set of new lighting: the old man had installed black lights, strobes, and a crystal ball dangled from the low ceiling. James saw Aidan standing by the turntable. "So, did you manage to pay off your debt?"

"Almost, Jimmy, and saved some, as well."

"You gonna stay in the village?"

"I've applied for school. Your face is looking well enough. She really gave you a good one!"

"You know about it?"

"Everyone does. How did it feel getting the handshake from the most intelligent girl in town?

"I'll tell you, Aidan, she can really pack a punch."

"She stopped by our house a few days ago. Asked to pick some songs for tonight. Old stuff."

"She wanted some old stuff. I found a few in my parents collection."

"Slow songs?"

"Some, also, some slow-beat ones. First time I ever heard them; my parents said it brought back memories of their courting days."

"Can't wait to hear. Any school in particular you want to go to?"

"Limerick University, but I don't know what I'll study."

"You'll figure it out, Aidan. If I don't see you again, good luck and best wishes."

"Thanks, Jimmy. I'll need it."

James went back to Bernadette, who was busy talking to her friends. Caroline and Ellsbeth surrounded her.

They all studied James' face. "Not too bad from a trained boxer."

"Does everybody know?"

"Of course," Caroline said. "Everybody in town does."

"Excuse me, while I step outside a moment," James said. Right out the door, his face against the snow. "WHAT THE FUCK, OVER!"

"What was that all about?" asked Harper.

"You wouldn't understand."

"We enjoyed our golf game with you fellas. Did Bernadette pay off?" She winked.

"Excuse me." He slipped back out into the cold, "WHAT THE FUCK, OVER!"

The music started playing. With the strobe lights flashing, everybody appeared to dance in slow motion. Not even tunes like "At The Hop" were fast enough. The sets alternated between fast and slow. At a break, Bernadette went to the bar and returned with pints for Caroline and Harper, then two bags of potato chips, one bag of pretzels, one pack of peanuts, and a ginger ale.

"We heard the good news," Harper said. "Do you want a boy or a girl?"

"I want a healthy baby."

"It's so thrilling! A baby, married soon, and house in Dingle. We're so happy for you!"

James thought about going out the door again. "I'm ready to dance."

A cheer went up when AC/DC played. They sang along with "Highway To Hell" and

"Have a Drink on Me." Raising their glasses, James thought they were singing the national anthem. James saw Harper and Caroline dancing together. The boys didn't approach them while dancing, except during a break.

Aidan bellowed out, "The Stroll!"

"The Stroll! They do that old dance in Ireland?"

Caroline and Harper closed, cheek to cheek, to "I Only Have Eyes For You." The Drifters' "Under the Boardwalk" started, and Bernadette led him to the Shag. They found themselves alone in the middle of the floor, others watching their steps and turns. "Where did you learn that dance?" Caroline asked Bernadette.

"Myrtle Beach. They call it the Shag—beach music."

"Can you teach me?"

"The night is almost over. I'll show you next time."

The crystal ball slowly turned for 'I Can't Live '. "You asked for this song?"

"I love it," she answered.

The night ended with "Magic Moment,— and they all cleared the dance floor for James and Bernadette, who danced cheek to cheek. Everybody cheered.

Out on the sidewalk and bundled in coats, they saw each other's breath. "So," James said to Caroline and Harper, "I notice you only dance with each other."

The girls, including Bernadette, smiled. Harper said, "Mr. Flaherty. We don't need men in our lives. Does that shock you?"

"As long as you love one another is all that matters."

They smiled broadly and kissed him on both cheeks. "We love you!"

It had stopped snowing but turned colder. They shivered home. Once undressed and in bed, James felt her cold legs. He felt her nipples press against his chest and held her tightly and rubbed her back until her body warmed. "Thank you, lady. Great time."

In the middle of the night, James saw a single NVA soldier charging him with a fixed bayonet. As he came closer and closer, James raised his arms to protect himself, waiting for the stabbing…He woke in a sweat.

messages

"How's your arm, Flaherty?" Mckenzie asked.

"Sore, but much better."

"We're truckin' over to Bearcat this afternoon. Be ready by 1500 hours."

"Wilco. Where's Ardal?"

"Tryin' to find those hootch maids sellin' pussy. I don't think he's goin' to find one, though. The lifers got 'em all locked up. Shea must be pretty horny."

"I guess he'll have to choke the chicken. I'll square away and be ready."

Lieutenant Sam, Doc Joyner, McKenzie, Ardal, and I gathered at our hootch. The humidity was back although the monsoon had ended. We knew drier air would come soon, and we would sleep better.

"Did you find what you were lookin' for?" McKenzie asked Ardal.

Ardal presented a sly smile, "The lifers got 'em locked up."

"You did!" I said. "You actually did it. How much did you pay?"

"Not much."

"Was she any good?"

"Not great; not bad."

McKenzie offered, "Don't you know bad pussy is better than no pussy?"

"Where did you find her?" Sam asked.

"Up near the mess hall. She's a KP worker."

"Let's change the subject. It's makin' me horny, and I don't need that right now."

"I just remembered something," Joyner brightened, "we've reached two-digit status."

"Yeah, we're two-digit midgets."

"I can't wait 'til one-digit," I said. "Especially the last week — six days and a wake-up."

"I miss Lee," McKenzie sadly added.

"This really is all for nothing," Ardal added. "I never realized how stupid this war is. For what? Defending freedom for Vietnam, Republic of."

"Stop," Sam interjected. "Our job now is to survive these last two months."

Doc said, "We have replacements now. I saw them at smart school."

"What's that?"

"A new program, Brigade, started. They'll spend six days for adjustment."

"That's new," I said. "What do they do?"

"I went there to administer the new toothpaste the green machine developed. They had to brush for thirty minutes without spitting. It's an enamel hardener."

"I wish they had that here when we came." McKenzie said.

"Do you remember those days before we went out in the field?"

I said, "How can I forget? We filled sandbags and hacked away the jungle for setup. My first shit burning detail; some sergeant from brigade picked Lee and me. 'Come with me; we're gonna burn some shit.' He took us to the latrine and handed us gloves and a paddle; told us to pull out the fifty-five gallon drums. Lee said, 'Wait a minute. This is SHIT! You said we're gonna' burn some shit, you know, like papers, files, and brushes. Not SHIT!'"

"What are you talking about, troop? What did you think we'd do?"

"Some shit, not SHIT!"

"We had to mix the stuff and pour kerosene in, mix again and light it with paper. Four barrels."

"I did that detail a lot," Joyner said.

"Let's concentrate on the mission before us. Bearcat overnight, then the mountains next day. It should be easy. Don't bring 'C's. The Thai's will set up food outlets."

"Are we going back to the 'ville after this?" Ardal asked.

Sam wiped sweat from his forehead. "I don't know."

"I miss it. I miss Lee."

"I do, too."

We got our shit together and quietly rested.

The two and a half trucks carried us to the junction of highways fifteen and twenty. Twenty led to the beaches of Vung Tau. A short ride later we turned right into Bearcat, a small encampment resting on a small hill overlooking a wide river. "See that river?" McKenzie pointed out, "That leads to the Rung Sat. The Thais operate there, the Queens Royal Cobra Regiment. How's that for a descriptive name?"

There were some empty barracks we could rest in. A small club sat nearby, and up the hill, the Thai's had set up a hamburger restaurant: handmade ground beef up to a full pound with buns and condiments.

Lieutenant Sam told Ardal, "We actually cleared this place before we moved to the Delta. Engineers plowed away the brush, and we hacked out the rest. It was meant for the Ninth Division advanced party, but when the whole division arrived, they moved to Dong Tam down in the Mekong."

"Then the Thais moved in?" Ardal asked.

"There are three major TCN's in Vietnam."

"What are TCN's?"

"Third Country Nationals. The Australians have a base camp down in Vung Tau; Koreans up at Cam Ram Bay. Soft areas, actually. Let's go up and get a burger before we settle in."

After eating the marvels of beef, they settled near the wooden buildings. I asked McKenzie, "Think we should do the final J here?"

"I don't think it's a good idea. Let's relax for tomorrow's hump."

"Yeah," I said to Ardal, "You can see the Nui Vai across the road. Nui Vai actually translates to 'shoulder mountain.' See that peak up there? That's where we're goin.'"

A small group of us congregated at the tiny EM Club, where we drank whiskey shots and beer. "I like the Ba Mui Ba beer." I savored the glass.

"Is it anything like Guinness?"

"I never had… what did you call it?"

"Guinness. Irish Stout."

"Maybe we don't carry it back in the States."

"There's a couple bars in Philadelphia that have it."

"I'll have to go to Philly and try it."

Now mellowed, we ended up lazing around the barracks for the rest of the day.

"Hey Ardal. What are you going to do back in the world?"

"I'm thinking about opening an Irish pub in Philly."

I said, "I'm going back to college in South Carolina."

"Me, too," McKenzie added. "Back in Maryland, seeking the ideal woman."

I said, "The ideal woman for me would be one who's intelligent and well-educated."

"What about her looks?"

"McKenzie, all women are beautiful in their own way, especially the intelligent ones."

Next morning, we crossed the highway to begin our ascent. "Lock and load," McKenzie ordered. Agent Orange had cleared most of the vegetation. We saw Vietnamese gathering small pieces of wood and loading carts with bamboo handles. I walked point, with Ardal pulling slack, armed with a grenade launcher loaded with a canister round. The canister had a hard plastic casing with twelve gauge buckshot. It was for stopping power and a good slack weapon.

We had to march in a single column; the mountain trail was too narrow for a double column. The familiar song came to my head, "Like an old dusty road, I get weary from the load; movin' on, movin' on like this tired, troubled earth, I've been roaming since my birth, movin' on, movin' on. There's a place in the sun where there's hope for everyone, and I'm gonna find that place in the sun." I couldn't get it out of my head ,no matter how hard I tried.

We sweated up the path, stopping for short breaks. We knew it was two miles, but all uphill, it seemed like five. Foliage reappeared high above, as the chemical had no effect here. I found a string with rotten C-ration cans still strung across the trail; 'Old, must have been here a long time, no longer useful to them.' Soon after, we came across the body of a North Vietnamese soldier; dead a long time, it had turned into cardboard, eaten out by critters. It didn't have that familiar, rotten stink of death. We passed it with notice. By now I was farther ahead of the squad and had been sweeping away overhanging branches from the narrow path. Near the summit, I ducked under a large one. Just then, I felt a sharp, burning pain in the back of my neck; a bullet flipped me around and onto the ground. *Maybe I found my place in the sun, oh no, not like this!* I was suddenly sleepy, but I struggled to keep my eyes open. I could feel the warm blood, and the pain was excruciating, like a red-hot poker across the back of my neck. I tried to raise my rifle, but boulders covered the side of the trail. A deep cliff fell off the other side. I couldn't find a target among the boulders. I found the M16's selector switch, but it wouldn't move. I pushed with my thumb as hard as I could, but the switch was frozen. I tried my left finger. Still no success. My right hand couldn't get it to move; nothing. I kept trying, but to no avail, then... I decided to get off the trail. I struggled to rise onto my knees; I gave up and fell flat. With all the strength I could muster, I rolled. Slow at first, then my momentum carried me off the edge. Another machine gun burst! It had to be point blank; the gas thumped! Nearing me, Ardal fired his canister round; it careened off the boulders. Then the firing at me stopped. The canister must have scared them away.

Sam, McKenzie, and Joyner hurried up while Ardal kept his position. Doc wrapped a green towel around my neck and pressed hard enough to stop the bleeding, but it didn't stop the burning pain. "Move your legs," Joyner barked.

"Morphine? It's gettin' worse."

"Not for head and neck wounds. Besides, you're going to have to hold on when they lift the penetrator."

"What's that?"

"The chopper can't land. They'll have to drop a penetrator seat to lift you."

"What the fuck, over."

Ardal moved up and put his arm around me. "Hang on, brother. I don't want to lose you."

Two gunships swooped in and sneezed rockets and fired their miniguns. They parted to allow the dust off in; they'd swing around for another pass after the medivac lifted off. Ardal, Doc, and McKenzie held my shoulders and pulled me to a standing position. I could hardly do it, my legs so wobbly. So they held on tightly. I still couldn't stand; my knees buckled. They held on tighter.

"We've gotta get you on that seat!" The towel around my neck was soaked.

They let the seat hit the ground. They helped me wrap my legs around it; less than two foot circumference, vibrating and swinging now; I grabbed on as it lifted me on the seat. A large tree branch snagged it, but I kicked my right leg and swung free. Above tree level, the chopper took off over a valley, suddenly two thousand feet below. Now the chain swung wider and wider as I gripped harder and harder to keep from falling to my death. Barely hanging on to the swinging seat as they hoisted me up, I rose level, and the medic pulled me into the medivac. The medic peeled off the bloody towel and tossed it out the open door and tightly wrapped a bandage. The chopper seemed to fly faster to the hospital tarmac. They wheeled me in on a gurney and laid me on my stomach in a bed. I rested on my chin, wondering what next. At the same time I was brought in, more casualties arrived, moaning and crying; I was triaged behind them. I could hear the turmoil, and talking among the surgeons and nurses. One nurse came to me, and rested her hand on the small of my back while a senior emergency room medic rubbed hot cream on my neck.

"What are you doin?" I asked.

"Debriding. I'm going to shave your hair near the wound. Bullets carry loads of bacteria with them. It won't hurt, but you'll have to wait here. Gotta get to the others first."

I tried to cover my ears against the screams and crying. About an hour later, the crying stopped, and the doctor finally got to me. He shot me full of xylocaine and started stitching. Then more xylocaine. "Damn," he said.

"What's wrong?"

"The skin connecting the head to the shoulder is the toughest. I'm breaking needles. be patient, sir."

It was another hour before he finished. "There. You'll be fine in a couple days. I'll visit you in the ward."

They sedated me well, and I went to sleep instantly, the pain subsiding. Next morning, a ward nurse came in and ordered all the patients out of the bed. "Not you, sir." She made them make their beds, inspected up and down, and ordered them back in bed.

Later that morning, a bird Colonel appeared and pinned the Purple Heart on my pillow and rendered a smart salute. The other patients stared; they were in for sickness, one with a rat bite. Maybe they hadn't seen a purple heart before. I hadn't either. Maybe the scorpion was not counted as an enemy.

The pain was better after three days. That afternoon, Sam, Joyner, and Ardal visited. "Feeling better, James?"

"Much. Where's McKenzie?"

"He had some paperwork. He'll stop by later."

Sam said, "Next time, duck."

"I did; thanks a lot!"

Ardal hugged me, tears in his eyes. "That was too close, brother."

"That flight was what almost got me. I could've fallen off."

"Brother, someone's watching over you; you must have some sort of purpose for God."

"I don't know about that. When are we going back to the 'ville?"

"A couple days, but you're not going with us."

"I don't want to be away from you guys. What are they going to do to me?"

Joyner smiled broadly. "Send you home."

"Wha-a-a?"

"You got a drop!" said Sam.

"Less than a week," Ardal said happily. "You're a one-digit midget now."

"Whoa. I'll need a step ladder to lace my boots."

Ardal's voice caught. "I'm gonna miss ya, brother. I'll see you in Philadelphia when

you get back home. Brothers, forever."

"Forever. Take care of yourself, Ardal. I want to try that Guinness you talked about."

"On the house."

It was raw outside and just beginning to rain. On the edge of the bed, Bernadette dropped the final notebook in her lap and choked back tears. He glanced up. "What's wrong, sweetie?"

Her head in her hands, James opened his arms and rested her head on his shoulder. "What's wrong?" He kissed her forehead and brushed away tears. "Please don't cry. I'm here."

"That's just it. You're here." She looked into his eyes. "When I first met you, I was dazzled, and the more I got to know you, the more I liked. "I'm so sad for your past, and so happy we're going to be married!"

"That's nothing to cry about."

"You don't understand. If you'd gotten killed, I would have never met you, and our life together would've died with you. That's what makes me so sad."

He hugged her again and kissed her and smiled. "That chapter in my life has long passed. I'm here. We're going to marry in two weeks and settle in a new house."

She said, "I love you so much. Please don't ever leave me."

"Let's finish packing. We'll go visit your family and say good bye."

She pulled herself together, and they finished the packing. They heard a tap on the front door. James opened it and saw Ollie, his short, red hair wet in the sleet. "Mr. Savage! What can I do for you?"

"I won't come in. I just came to congratulate you and Bernadette."

Bernadette stepped behind James. "Thanks, Ollie."

"I won't bother you," Ollie continued. "My respects. I decided to go to Omagh."

"I thought you liked Dunmore East."

"Maybe I'll come back, but my future is with my friend there."

James peered into Ollie's blue eyes and wondered about his change of heart; perhaps Ollie was finally facing reality and had given up his scheming. "Thanks, Ollie. I appreciate it."

Ollie walked to the curb, and they watched him get into his car and pull away.

"I don't trust him," she said. "He's a cute hoor."

"What's that?"

"Somebody who arranges things to his own advantage."

"He seemed sincere to me."

"He's a jagoff."

Bundled up against the weather, they drove to the inn. There were only a few guests now. Her mother widened her eyes. "You children ready to leave?"

"Soon," James said. "Where's Jack?"

"He went to town on business."

"Will he be back before we leave? We can't wait too long."

"Bernadette," Delany said, "Your dad's very proud of you, and he loves your fiancée, but I don't think he can stand seeing you two leave."

"We'll wait," James said. "We really want to see him."

"Let's go and see my sister," Bernadette said. "We'll come back, Mum."

Moira and Tony had been waiting to send them off. Bernadette hugged her sister, "I love you, sis."

"We love you," her eyes damp. Tony shook James hand. "I'd like to visit after you two settle. I've always wanted to play Ballybunion. And the Dooks."

"I'd like that," James answered. "We can all play together."

* * *

Back at the inn, Jack was still absent. "We have to leave," Bernadette said. "It's getting late, and the rain."

Sighing, "I guess your father's 'up to the nineties'" They kissed and hugged then they got back in the VW and went to load their bags. Then they went straightaway.

As she drove past the crystal factory, Bernadette pointed to the rundown neighborhood across the road. "My life began there."

"Awful. How could you stand it?"

"I was too young. We moved to Dunmore East."

"Good move."

An hour went by before they reached Clonmel, then into County Cork, where they passed a double rainbow. The rain had stopped, and they passed villages and towns. She slowed down for roundabouts, and James was glad they skipped Cork City, as he had never liked the traffic; too busy and confusing. They sped west toward Tralee. "Would you slow down?" James worried, "The garda might pull us over."

"We left late. We'll never make it to Dingle tonight. I know a short cut through Tralee."

"Can't you go around?" She made a sharp turn, and at length James saw the iron statue of Puck, the goat celebrated at the Rose of Tralee festival. On into town, they came upon a slow jam. Then they came to a stop. "Bumper to bumper." she sighed.

"You better turn off the engine. We might be a while."

"I don't know what's going on. Maybe an accident."

"Must be a long way ahead."

People began stepping out of their houses. A man approached them. "Accident on the other side of town. Minor injuries. They have to clear away a lorry and a tractor until you can move. Like to use my facilities?"

"Oh yes. My teeth are floating!"

The man burst into laughter. "Follow me."

James took his turn after she hurried back to the car. Half an hour later, the cars began to move, but very slowly. She restarted and pushed the gear into first. "Finally."

"I'll say: Finally, fuckin' finally, fuckin' finally."

"You don't have to be so crude."

"Crude? What about your floating teeth? Now, that was crude."

"Normal body functions."

"We gonna keep fussin' or move ahead?"

Her foot still on the clutch, "I'm trying to. As soon as this jam breaks up."

"There. We're starting to move."

She groaned, "Finally fuckin,' finally fuckin,' finally!"

They laughed and high-fived.

Leaving the outskirts of town, "Getting dark now," she worried, "I hope we can find a place for the night."

"Do you know of any?"

"I've only passed through this place. Entering the town of Killorglin, rounding a curve past Saint James Cathedral, down the hill she saw the Kingston House. "There. Maybe there. It's winter. Maybe we can get in."

The smell of pizza greeted them as they entered, and revelers crowded the bar. "Pizza!" she cheered, "I want some!"

"Let's see if we can find a room first."

A man approached, "Seeking accommodations?"

"Yes," James answered, "one night. Do you have vacancy?"

"I have a room still available. Follow me." He led them down a hallway to room 104; "Now then. This should be appropriate for you and the missus."

"Excellent," Bernadette replied. "We'll take it. Mr. and Mrs. Flaherty."

"Very well. Let's get you registered."

"Could you unlock the room for her while I register at the desk?"

"We're having pizza tonight if you'd like to join us."

"My wife and I love pizza. It smells great."

They managed to find one small table close to the bar where James ordered a pint, while she ordered pizza. They leaned back in their chairs; it'd been a long day.

The pizza arrived hot and sizzling along with the Guinness.

James took a slice and rolled it into a tube.

"What are you doin?"

"Fixin' my pizza, Pittsburgh style."

"I never saw that before." Tomato sauce dripped on her chin. She wiped it and continued. "Pittsburgh has some strange habits."

"Only if you go down town."

The pizza was excellent, and they enjoyed the warm atmosphere until, finished and satisfied, they returned to their room.

Undressed, they lay down on the soft bed. She sighed, "I'm so excited about finding our new home."

"I am, too. But first, I have to do my duty: pay respects to my brother in arms."

"Are you going to cry when you see Ardal's grave?"

"I don't know, but it's my duty."

They passed the night in each other's arms, dreaming about the future.

Next morning, James stood near the open window in the bathroom. He heard morning traffic on Killorglin's streets, and people talking. He thought about Ardal and tried to imagine Ardal's family living here. He remembered the Irishman mentioning Glenveigh and his uncle's pub there. And Dingle Bay. He went back to the bed and kissed Bernadette. She stirred. "We should leave soon," he told her.

She stretched. "What time is it?"

"Just daylight. We can see Ardal's grave and get to Dingle before noon if we leave soon."

They dressed and went to the bar and had coffee. "Look, James. Continental breakfast. Very European."

They ate croissants and fruit. She enjoyed the smoked salmon and cream cheese. She paused and sat up straight, "So, how are you feeling about visiting Ardal?"

"Nervous. It's been so long."

"I feel like I know him, you described him so well."

"You ready?"

They ascended the hill leading to the cathedral. "Saint James was built in the 900s." She read off a card.

They entered the gate and circled the church to the expansive cemetery. They looked at one another and shrugged. "I think we should spread out," she said.

Among gravestones they searched, reading names and dates from long ago. After thirty minutes, James, beginning to doubt his mission, sighed, "Maybe we should have gone inside and searched the registry." Bernadette called to him from a newer section, and they continued up and down the rows of newer granite stones. "Hey, look, James! Here he is!"

He saw a light gray stone marker. Ardal Peter Shea. Born August fifth, 1946; Died January Fourteen, 1968. Tears welled in his eyes, and Bernadette put her arm around him and squeezed. He whispered, "Well, my brother, I finally found you. I wish we were still together. Maybe I could've saved you again, like I did when you were drowning. We had some good times together, and guess what? I'm going to live near you. I met a wonderful Irish girl, a school teacher, and we're going to live in Dingle. I'm a gentleman of means, and there won't be a day in my life that I won't think of you. Someday I'll join you. Goodbye until then." His tears fell.

Bernadette wiped his eyes with a Kleenex, then wiped hers. She said. "I guess we should go."

They decided to go to confession before they left. James came out of the cathedral and waited for her. He walked around the corner, where he found a low stone wall for sitting. She came out after forty-five minutes. "Over here!" James waved. "Why did it take you so long?"

"Let's go back to Kingston's and drive home."

On the sidewalk in front of the bakery window, James said, "I'm going to love…."

A sharp, sudden pain in his lower back, and he fell to his knees. Startled, Bernadette saw the blood staining the back of his shirt and screamed. He collapsed, onto his side. Shop owners came out to see. Bernadette clung to him.

"I called ambulance," the woman from the cleaners said. "How is he?"

A man checked under the shirt. "It looks like gunshot; small caliber. Who could have done this?"

James groaned, "No, not like this."

Bernadette turned away and gagged, then she wailed wide-open to the sky. More people arrived, and another man held a towel on James' back and pressed. He began to lose consciousness.

Ambulance came screeching. Emergency techs dashed out and rushed to James, then lifted him, face down on a stretcher and loaded him in.

"I'm going with him!" Bernadette shouted, and climbed in.

It took only minutes to reach the emergency room in Tralee, but James' breathing became labored and then very quiet. The medic kept pressing his back as the blood oozed, and the other ETM, a young woman, revealed a defibrillator ready. It started raining a fine mist. The siren shrieked as Bernadette crouched, shaking, until they reached the emergency room at Bons Secours.

Inside the hospital, the woman medic asked her, "Can I do anything for you? I can give you something that'll calm your nerves."

"I only want my husband!"

From the emergency room, the doctor came out to consult with the medic. She had blood on her gown.

"We're going to operate."

Bernadette's tears ran.

"Don't worry, Madam," the medic said, sharing what the doctor had told her. "They're having a hard time getting the bullet out. She said it must've been a hollow point; the round collapsed into three pieces. I'll take you up to the surgery waiting area."

In the waiting room next to the surgery, Bernadette settled in a chair and saw through the window rain streaming down the pane. After an hour, rain continuing, she clutched her rosary and prayed, lips trembling. A priest arrived and went on through the double doors, but emerged and quickly left. More staff hurried by her and entered the surgery. She went back to her rosary and closed her eyes as the rain eased a bit. Shortly after, she noticed sunrays peeking brightly through the mist. Her eyes full of tears, Bernadette gripped her Rosary and thought, *He's with Ardal now.*

Exhausted, she asked the EMT who had stayed in the hospital, waiting for her, if she could take her back to Kingston's in Killorglin. "Of course," she smiled, "I know Erwin and Chroi well. They're good people. I'd be happy to."

Back at the hotel after the ride back, Bernadette sat near the bar and had a lime mineral. She had finished phone calls to her mother and sister, telling them the awful news. Her tears had dried, and she stared across the table, *I bear his child. I'll have to make sure it grows strong. I know I will see him in heaven.*

Perhaps I'll join him with Ardal by his side. In fact, I'll join my family and friends up there. We'll be together and live happily in Paradise. She placed her head in her hands and wept.

* * *

Free falling. The penetrator seat swayed above him. He wondered how it would feel crashing onto the ground: Would it be quick? his bones would break; his head would split open. He hoped it would be quick. Then…his body turned, and he found himself flying. Just in time to sail upward, alongside a brightly colored bird, wings steady, above the trees, over the boulders, he turned on his back to look up into the sky and saw more colorful birds around him. He rolled again, plunged to the tree tops, and sailed again. Up and down, up and down, and the chain twisting above him, the helicopter battered by the winds above him, it turned and shook. He saw the seat and stretched, stretched, stretched to it. New stars brightly rose and mounds of dust in the shapes of human bodies drifted like a moonscape. He heard his mother and father call, "Jimmy." Dust disappeared to reveal the bodies: young men neatly arranged in the order of their deaths, the struggle between Ba Hoa, the fire goddess, and the evil Ma Da, water ghosts, drowning in the darkness. Polaris flashed brighter and brighter, pulling him into the fire. He felt his blood warming, then chilling; fingers and toes tingling. Conflagration swirled and encompassed. Silhouettes of women with tearful, darkened eyes—Ellsbeth, Harper, and Caroline, holding hands and kissing. Moira was setting a pint down, wiping her eyes. Another form, much larger and emerging from the light, revealed Ardal. Hair silver and eyes familiar Stretched his arm and pushed hard. Smiled and faded into the light. Then darkness again.

"Mr. Flaherty, wake up. Can you hear me?"

"Oh-h-h. Who are you?"

"I'm your ICU nurse. Can you see me?"

"Yes. What happened?"

"Welcome back, Mr. Flaherty. Welcome back. My name is Cliodhna, your nurse. The doctor's going to come and see you. You'll be with us a couple of days. Be careful not to turn on that bandage."

"Bandage?"

"Where you were shot. It's going to be sore for a while. Are you hungry?"

"Lamb kidneys braised in red wine."

Cliodhna laughed. "We don't have that here! How about some broth and a cup of Jello?"

"If you insist. Where's my wife?"

"She left."

"My wife. Bernadette. Where did she go?"

"I'll have to check on that, Mr. Flaherty. She left and came back. The medic took her to Killorglin."

"Oh, no! She could be going back to Dunmore East to be with her family!"

"Do you have other family here, Mr. Flaherty?"

"Just the Bohans. They live in Dunmore East." She said I'm about to get off, Mr. Flaherty.

"Where did she go in Killorglin?"

"Kingstons."

"I know the Kingstons. I'll go straightaway!" She then rushed to the cathedral, the Kingstons having told her where Bernadette was going.

* * *

Hail Mary, full of grace, the Lord is with thee; blessed art thou among women, and blessed is the fruit of thy womb, Jesus, Holy Mary, mother of God, pray for us sinners now and at the time of our death. Amen. Behold the handmaid of the Lord: be it done unto me according to Thy word.

I could have stopped it. Why didn't I? I should have put Ollie in the hospital when I had the chance. He's evil and psychotic.

Hail Mary, full of grace, the Lord is with thee; blessed art thou among women, and blessed is the fruit of the womb, Jesus, Holy Mary, mother of God, pray for us sinners now and at the time of our death. Amen. Behold the handmaid of the Lord: be it done unto me according to Thy word.

I let James down. My husband, the father of my child. I failed him after the others saved him. I must ensure our child will grow strong in his name!

Our Father, who art in heaven, hallowed be thy name; Thy kingdom come; Thy will be done on earth as it is in heaven. Give us this day our daily bread; and forgive us our trespasses as we forgive those who trespass against us; and lead us not into temptation, but deliver us from evil.

I will be here through the night. I will be here through tomorrow. And next night, next day. Our father—

"Mrs. Flaherty, I'm Cliodhna from the hospital. Your husband's alive!"

dingle

After Sunday Mass, the Flaherty's enjoyed the carvery at an old hotel in Dingle Town. Bernadette fussed over little Charlie, wiping his chin and cutting his meat into small pieces. James said, "He can eat by himself."

"I'm afraid he might stab himself. He grips the fork with his fist."

James II (aka Jimmy), now fourteen; Cliodhna, twelve; and Antoinette, eight, handled themselves well at the dinner table. They helped one another.

"See that floor space over there, James."

"Oh, yes."

"Wouldn't it make a grand dance floor?"

"For disco?"

"For shag."

"Nobody around here knows that dance."

"But we could teach them. We can start a shag club!"

"That might work. Will you set it up?"

"Sure."

"Wednesdays?"

"Wednesdays," she said.

"You're so sentimental."

James added, "I liked how you set up our French restaurant, Lamont By The Sea, a great idea."

"Profitable, too. I'm thinking about an Italian one: Il Divino."

"You have great business sense."

"And you have the money."

"I'd like to take Jimmy to Kinsale soon. The Irish Veterans Association is established there. Maybe we might meet the Shea family."

"I sent them your memoir a long time ago. You might find out how they received it. And James, you found her."

"Who?"

"That perfect woman you talked about before you got wounded."

"Dad," said Jimmy, "are you going to tell me about the war?"

"In time, son. When you're a wee bit older, I'll let you read my memoir and answer any questions. Except for having you and your brother and sisters, it was the most important experience of my life."

"I'd like that."

Bernadette pondered awhile. "You know, James. School's out for the summer. We should take the kids on a trip overseas."

"Great idea. We could retrace ours in the States."

"Grand! It'll help with their horizons."

"Do you want me to make arrangements?"

Bernadette said, "Please do."

"With all this development going on, our land is much more valuable."

"Maybe we should sell."

"Not yet," James said. "When the kids leave home, we could sell for much more and find a place in town."

Bernadette chuckled. "Your yinzer is still with you."

"A slip."

Cliodhna piped in. "What's yinder?"

"Yinzer, darling. You're dad used to speak it until he learned Irish."

"Funny."

"Very funny," James added.

Turning to James, "I've been thinking about Ollie," Bernadette quietly said.

"Why?"

"I heard he's getting early release from prison."

"I guess that's good."

"You remember when we testified at his trial? I suggested he be put in a psych ward, but the judge denied it. He received his mental health in prison."

"Hopefully he's better," James added. "I don't want him to shoot me again."

* * *

The kids watched the Carolina countryside skim by. The divided highway awed them; right side driving stunned them. "Mom," Antoinette said. "Why do we drive the left side?"

"We always used the right side," James said. "I grew up driving this way. I had to relearn driving in Ireland."

The O'Leary's did live in the same house and were expecting them. James and Bernadette gathered the kids and knocked on the front door. She saw through the glass the large deck where years ago the cookout was held. She remembered the dancing and smiled.

Sadie opened the door. "Surprise!"

"Lordy, Lordy! It's been a long time, y'all. And look at your young guns! Beautiful! Let's decide who looks like who. Thomas! They're here!"

"So glad you called from Charlotte. What a surprise! How about a beer?"

"That would be great, thanks," Bernadette said.

Tom handed her a can of Bud Light. She took a sip and winced.

"You don't like It?"

"Oh yes." She lied. "Excuse me, I forgot something in the van and came back holding a straw bag.

"Would you watch the kids while Jim and I go out on the deck?"

"Sure," Sadie and Tom replied.

Bernadette led James by the hand. She turned to him, "Remember when we danced on this deck?"

"As the Southerners say. Hell no, I ain't forgettin.' "

"We really threw down that night."

She smiled while reaching into the bag. "Here, a gift for you." She handed him a cell phone.

"What's this?"

"A phone. I have one, too.

He handled it and said, "How do we call on this?"

"Now we can talk to each other from a distance. We can text and email."

"What are you saying? Text and email?"

"New form of communication, James. Our children will enter a new world of technology. Think of it."

"Amazing. Show me."

She tapped a few times and spelled out a song. Miracle. Music. THIS MAGIC MOMENT! She gently pulled him closer, and they danced cheek to cheek.

She touched his chest and felt his pulse. "My heart is within you."

* * *

Bernadette reclaimed her sitting spot under the umbrella on the beach. She was wearing shorts and a cotton blouse. She watched James and the kids. The little ones wore water wings. Jimmy and Cliodhna were old enough to swim. They splashed around with their father. Charlie played with a sand pail and shovel. She knew the children had found their connection. Between Dingle Bay and the warm, rolling sea in South Carolina instilled in them that connection.

She thought what a marvel Evolution was. It was God's miracle, indeed. With the salt connection, human evolution began in the sea from amphibians to mammals. There were creatures who had both gills and lungs; they progressed to birds, to dinosaurs.

All the creatures leading to man shared hollow bones, a prerequisite for the human body structure.

James returned to sit on the shaded sand next to her. He'd instructed Jimmy and Cliodhna to watch over the little ones and help Charlie with his sand castle. He sat and launched his thousand-yard stare to the horizon.

Bernadette said, "Thinking about Ardal?"

"Yes, and the others. I can never get it out of my mind why I survived and they didn't."

"What about those who did survive? The Lieutenant, the medic, Makenzie, and Lorenzo. Do you think about them, too?"

"Just those that didn't survive."

They sat quietly a while. Bernadette put her hand on his arm. "Listen James. I think you have it all wrong. You shouldn't feel guilty."

"I can't help it."

"You need to consider some things," she said. "Remember when you saved Ardal from drowning; you told God he's yours, not his. It was as if you'd crossed the Jordan. The medic was baptized again, changed his outlook, and decided to carry a weapon."

"Don't you see that Ardal and God answered you? When you almost died, they intervened and brought you back to life, a new life. Do you understand? Look at your little ones on that beach. Look at our life in Dingle; your dedication to Irish Veterans. You made us well off, allowing us to be here and enjoy our extended family. Look at yourself, swallowed with sorrow and pity. Well, look again!

"And our restaurant is thriving. The Shag club became popular. Look at me. Don't ruin it with your self-pity. You're blessed by God. You have everything you need for a happy life. Don't waste it."

James gazed into her eyes. "I'm so glad I have you."

She kissed his cheek and squeezed his hand. "Let's gather up our kids and go get some seafood, Mister Irishman."

* * *

A few days later in Pennsylvania, they stopped at Judy Jessep's house, surprising her again. JJ opened her arms, "I can't believe it! You two, and those kids. Adorable." She opened the door wide. "Come in, come in. Let's see who the kids favor."

The family moved indoors. Bernadette ushered the bigger ones and picked up Charlie and held him in her arms.

JJ said, "You kids sit on that couch." One of her many cats leapt up and purred on Antoinette's lap for pets. "Let's see. Tell ya the truth; I can't see who! I think the oldest favors you, Bernadette."

"I don't see where any of our wans favor anyone but the both of us."

"Waynes? What's that?"

"Children."

"Hey, Judy. Why don't you show the kids your animals?"

"The animals! They're drivin' me crazy now. You know them groundhogs are multiplyin.' I can hardly keep up with their food. C'mon kids." She led them to the front porch and pointed under.

"Those are big," Jimmy exclaimed and pulled back.

"Let's go to the backyard," JJ said. "I'll show ya where the racoons are.

See that thick bush over there? That's where they live. You can't see them 'til they come out at night. There's three of 'em."

"Do you still see Marlin up the alley?" James asked.

"Oh. Let me tell ya, Jim. He turned into a real jagoff."

"I always thought he was a nice guy."

"Was. C'mon kids. Let's get you something to eat. Do you like pop?"

"What's that?" Antoinette asked. "And is she speaking yinder?"

"Yinzer. She sure is."

"Pop is the same as minerals," their mother said.

JJ said, "I still love your accent. And Jim is getting one, too."

"Enculturation," James answered.

"I can make you sandwiches. How 'bout some chips or pretzels?"

"Just some...pop..." Bernadette answered for them.

"So what are you gonna do when you get into town?"

"I'm not sure yet. I'd like them to see the sights."

"You stayin' at the William Penn again?"

"Yes," James and Bernadette replied in unison.

JJ thought a few minutes before saying, "You know what would be good for the kids? The museum of natural history and the planetarium on the north side. Then you can take them to Kennywood."

"What's Kennywood?" Bernadette asked.

"An amusement park. They still have those old-fashioned roller coasters. Kiddieland offers rides for the little ones. And there's the Ferris wheel and merry-go-round. You can pass the steel mill and the Russian Orthodox Church."

"I'd like for them to ride the Incline like James and I did."

"That'll give you enough to do."

"Well, Judy, I think it's time. Thanks for everything."

"When do you think you'll be back?"

"I really don't know, but maybe with the kids when they get older."

* * *

They settled in at the William Penn. James put Jimmy and Cliodhna in charge of the little ones with a kids show on TV, while he and his wife rested. They made it easy and ate in the hotel. Hamburgers and chips. James and Bernadette had Iron Cities.

Early next morning, they took a cab to the Incline, riding both ways. "When we get back to the bottom, can I get another hamburger like I ate last night?" The kids loved it, and they accomplished everything they set out to do. They even ate Turkey Devonshire.

Two days later they boarded the flight to Shannon. The kids filled up a four seat row, and James and Bernadette took the seats across. As the plane climbed into and through the clouds, Bernadette said, "James, I think we should do two things when we get home. A reunion for all our families and friends, including the Shea's and the Powers.' I'll make the arrangements. May fifth every year."

"Why May fifth?"

"That was the day I first met you. It should be fun."

"Perfect. What else?"

"I think we should take some time alone. I'm sure their grandparents and aunt would be delighted to bring the cousins and stay with our children."

"Where shall we go?"

"Killorglin. We can visit Ardal's grave and stay at the Kingston's. We can play Ballybunion and the Dooks."

"P & P? Maybe Erwin and Chroi can book us room 104. Where do you want to hold the reunion?"

"Adare Manor."

"Maybe we could play golf there; maybe Lahinch, too." She rested her head on his shoulder, and they flew on east through the clouds.

THE END

ACKNOWLEGEMENTS

During three years of research, I "Had" to return to Ireland two more times. I'd like to thank Kingston Townhouses in Killorglin: Erwin and Chroi, Glenn and Donal. And Lawrence and 'Mags' Hogan from Mid-Kerry Cab and tours.

Silver Tassie in Letterkenny: I didn't meet the owners, but wonderful staff, especially Teresa Sweeny.

The Woodfield House in Limerick: Donal Mulcahy, Lianne, Glen and Nancy. Always wonderful craic!

                                      Thank you all, and God Bless.

The Mekong Delta story is dedicated to Timothy R. Kessler, and the Irish men and women who served my country in Vietnam.

The Dunmore East story is dedicated to the Boland Family, owners and operators of the former Candlelight Inn.

Rain on the leaves is the tears of joy from the girl whose boy comes home from the war..............

                                                PHAM DUY, 1968

ABOUT THE AUTHOR

Born in Pittsburgh, Pa, **Richard Blaney** graduated from the University of South Carolina with a degree in International Studies. He's a certified working chef, and a serious student of history. He lives with his wife Ann in Columbia, South Carolina.

www.ingramcontent.com/pod-product-compliance
Lightning Source LLC
LaVergne TN
LVHW021815060526
838201LV00058B/3404